PENGUIN BOOKS

ELVIS OVER ENGLAND

Barry Hines was born in the mining village of Hoyland Common, near Barnsley, South Yorkshire. He was educated at Ecclesfield Grammar School, where his main achievement was to be selected to play for the England Grammar schools' football team. On leaving school, he worked as an apprentice mining surveyor and played football for Barnsley (mainly in the A team), before entering Loughborough Training College to study Physical Education. He taught for several years in London and South Yorkshire before becoming a full-time writer.

He is the author of eight other novels, including *A Kestrel for a Knave*, *The Blinder*, *Looks and Smiles* and *The Heart of It*. Both *A Kestrel for a Knave* (as *Kes*) and *Looks and Smiles* have been filmed, the latter winning the Prize for Contemporary Cinema at the Cannes Film Festival. He has also written many scripts for television, including *Threads*, which won the BAFTA award and the Broadcasting Press Guild Award for the best single drama.

Barry Hines is a Fellow of the Royal Society of Literature and an Honorary Fellow of Sheffield Hallam University.

Elvis Over England

Barry Hines

PENGUIN BOOKS

PENGUIN BOOKS

Published by the Penguin Group
Penguin Books Ltd, 27 Wrights Lane, London w8 5TZ, England
Penguin Putnam Inc., 375 Hudson Street, New York, New York 10014, USA
Penguin Books Australia Ltd, Ringwood, Victoria, Australia
Penguin Books Canada Ltd, 10 Alcorn Avenue, Toronto, Ontario, Canada M4V 3B2
Penguin Books (NZ) Ltd, Private Bag 102902, NSMC, Auckland, New Zealand

Penguin Books Ltd, Registered Offices: Harmondsworth, Middlesex, England

First published by Michael Joseph 1998
Published in Penguin Books 1999
10 9 8 7 6 5 4 3 2 1

Copyright © Barry Hines, 1998
The Acknowledgements on pp. vii–x constitute an extension of this copyright page

Set in Monotype Fournier
Printed in England by Clays Ltd, St Ives plc

To Eleanor

Acknowledgements

The author and publishers would like to thank the following for permission to use copyright material:

Carlin Music:
'Blue Suede Shoes', words and music by Carl Lee Perkins, © 1956 Hi-Lo Music Inc.
'Don't Be Cruel (To A Heart That's True)', words and music by Otis Blackwell and Elvis Presley, © 1956 Elvis Presley Music Inc. & Shalimar Music Inc.
'It's Now Or Never', words and music by Aaron Schroeder and Wally Gold, © 1960 Gladys Music Inc.
'Jailhouse Rock', words and music by Jerry Leiber and Mike Stoller, © 1957 Elvis Presley Music Inc.
'Love Me Tender', words and music by Elvis Presley and Vera Matson, © 1956 Elvis Presley Music Inc.

The bearers were lowering the coffin when the telephone rang. The sound was so incongruous that the mourners raised their heads and looked round, wondering what it was. The vicar just stood there, praying silently that the ringing would stop. But when it continued, he reached under his cassock and took out his mobile phone from his pocket.

'Hello,' he said, his gaze still fixed on the committal service.

'It's from God,' one of Eddie's young nephews whispered, loud enough for everyone to hear.

The other children giggled and the adults avoided each other's eyes to stop themselves from laughing. The boy's mother thumped him so hard in the back that he overbalanced and she had to grab his Boston Red Sox bomber jacket to prevent him toppling forward into the open grave.

Eddie looked down at the suspended coffin and thought that his mother deserved better.

When the service was over, and family and friends lingered tearfully at the grave side, embracing each other and reading the messages of condolence on the floral tributes, Eddie wandered away towards the older section of the cemetery and started to read the headstones. He thought he would find the grave immediately, but it was years since he had been and he soon lost his bearings. Then, as he turned towards the chimes of an ice-cream van playing 'Just One Cornetto', he looked down and saw the headstone. The inscription read:

IN LOVING MEMORY
JEFFREY JONES
1941–1960
A CANDLE TOO SOON SNUFFED OUT

Jeffrey . . . It sounded strange, a different person. Only his parents had called him by his proper name. His friends called him Jeff, until he metamorphosed into Jet after seeing *Rock Around the Clock* and buying his first Teddy-boy suit. And Jet he remained, from the Brylcreemed quiff of his duck's arse hairstyle, down to the thick crêpe soles of his blue suede shoes. Jet. Jet . . . The leader of the pack. Not much of a pack really, just Jet and Eddie for most of the time.

Eddie tidied the grave. He picked up a Coke can and some waste paper then pulled up the weeds and smoothed out the marble chippings. The flower vase had disappeared, so he walked across to the rubbish dump and found a milk bottle amongst the discarded wreaths and flowers. He filled it at the tap outside the Chapel of Remembrance, then returned to Jet's grave and settled it into the chippings near the headstone. He looked round for something to put in it. There were the dandelions which he had cleared from the grave. But they seemed inappropriate somehow, even disrespectful. A bunch of dandelions in a milk bottle was more fitting for a pet hamster's grave at the bottom of the garden.

'It's about time somebody tidied that grave up. It's a disgrace.'

Eddie turned towards an elderly woman tending a nearby plot.

'Yeah . . . Both his parents are dead and he had no brothers or sisters, that's the trouble. I'll try and come round myself a bit more often. We were best mates when we were young.'

'Yes, so were we.' She attacked the soil with the hand fork. 'Until we got married.'

Eddie laughed.

'You wouldn't be laughing if he'd been your husband, I can tell you.'

She struggled to her feet and dabbed the sweat from her face with a handkerchief.

'I'm sorry . . .'

'I'm not. They've been the best years of my life since he passed away.'

She dropped the fork into her handbag and walked away. Eddie considered doing her a favour by transferring the spray of fresh carnations from the grave of her hated husband on to Jet's plot, but she saw a friend grieving on a bench a few yards away and sat down to console her. Thwarted,

Eddie broke off a stem of fireweed growing behind Jet's headstone and stuck it in the milk bottle. With its long stalk and pointed head, it looked like a sky rocket.

Eddie stood back and appraised his work. It wasn't *Gardeners' World*, but it was a start, and he resolved to visit the grave regularly and keep it in good order. He stared at the crimson flower angling up out of the neck of the milk bottle and remembered a suit he used to have in the same shade of red. He was standing with his hands by his sides, comparing the length of his current suit jacket with the finger-tip length of the jackets he wore as a teenager, when his wife Pearl came up behind him.

'What are you doing?'

Eddie whipped round, startled and embarrassed.

'Nothing. What do you mean?'

'Standing to attention. You looked like a soldier.'

'If you fetch me a bugle, I'll play the Last Post.'

Pearl smiled and linked his arm. Her eyes were swollen and red from crying.

'We're going now. They're not all coming to the pub. I thought you might like to say cheerio.'

Eddie shaded his eyes with his hand and looked back across the cemetery. It was so hot that the mourners shimmered out of focus as they walked away.

'Yes. OK.' He looked down at Jet's grave. 'I just thought I'd tidy it up while I was here. I couldn't find it at first, it's that long since I've been.'

Pearl smiled at the flower in the milk bottle.

'You should have asked me. I knew where it was.'

Eddie shook his arm free and stepped away from her.

'Yeah, well. You would wouldn't you?'

4

'And what's that supposed to mean?'

Eddie stared wildly at Jet's grave. Pearl feared for the bottle. A peacock butterfly landed on the fireweed and opened its velvety wings.

'Fucking typical!' Eddie roared at it. 'If it had been my grave, it'd have been a cabbage white!'

Pearl smiled, her cheeks twitching nervously as she tried to placate him.

'I meant it's near that angel.' She pointed at a praying marble angel on a plinth. 'It's a landmark. I knew it was near his grave.'

She spoke quickly, trying to cap his temper before it erupted. Eddie turned away and stomped across the graves towards the path.

'Eddie! Where you going?'

He ignored her and kept on walking. When he reached the main entrance to the cemetery, he stopped and spoke to a gang of children playing on the wrought-iron gates. Pearl was too far away to hear what he said to them, but they immediately jumped down and walked away. They kept glancing back at him but there was no back-chat or abuse. Nobody talked back to Eddie.

As Eddie walked across the council estate to his mother's house, the back of his neck felt as if it was being burned through a magnifying glass. He mopped his face and loosened his tie, and when he took off his jacket, the sunlight was so intense on his white shirt that he couldn't bear to look down at it. Two fly boys, one black, one white, doing deals into mobiles outside a burned-out house, watched Eddie approach. They finished their conversations and the black guy stepped back, grinning and shielding his face as if Eddie was an exploding bomb.

'You look like the Daz advert, man!'

'New improved?'

'Definitely!'

Eddie took off the white guy's sunglasses and put them on.

'I could do with a pair of these in this weather.'

The black guy took off his baseball cap and jammed it on Eddie's head.

'It suits you, man. Cool!'

They all laughed. Eddie had become a split personality: Mister Straight Guy meets Dodgy Dude. He handed back the cap and sunglasses. The white guy winked at him before hiding his eyes behind his wraparounds.

'Anything you want, Eddie, you know where to come: caps, shirts, trousers, trainers . . .'

He pointed out each item on his partner, who slunk along the pavement and pivoted like a model.

The white guy stepped in close.

'We've just branched out into counterfeit, if you're interested. Double your money, if you see what I mean.'

Eddie laughed.

'You're wasting your talents here, you two. You should be down London, in the City. You'd make a fortune.'

He walked away, smiling and shaking his head. The black guy called his name and Eddie stopped and turned round.

'Sorry to hear about your mother.'

The white guy nodded in agreement.

'She was a really nice person. Everybody round here liked her.'

Eddie had to clear his throat before he could answer.

'Thanks, lads. I appreciate it.'

He walked away, wiping his eyes, then glanced up towards the blare of sirens in the distance. The noise grew louder, then overwhelmed him, as a police car, followed by an ambulance, appeared round the corner and rushed past. Eddie walked through the sound storm without wincing or turning round. He would have gone deaf rather than give the police the satisfaction of looking impressed.

He reached the end of the road, then turned into Byron Avenue. For a moment, he thought that the crowd at the far end of the avenue had gathered outside his mother's house and he started to run. But as he drew closer, he could see that they were standing a few doors further down, outside Harry Doyle's. He slowed down, drenched with sweat, and looked across at his mother's house with its drawn curtains and orphaned pot plants on the window ledge. Eddie couldn't help but laugh when he pushed through the crowd and saw what had happened. The privet hedge had been flattened and a car lay upside down on the front lawn like a beached whale. Betty Doyle was standing at the gate, explaining what had happened, but when she saw Eddie, she smiled and began the story again for his sake.

'I was just saying, Eddie, I was watching the telly, when there was such a crash outside I nearly had a heart attack. I thought the house was falling down or something. I couldn't believe it when I looked through the window and saw this lot,' pointing at the car. 'It's not every day you have a car crash on your front lawn, is it?'

The onlookers shook their heads in agreement and a few murmured, 'No.' They had seen other vehicles in puzzling places before. There was the occasion when Dean Barton's motor bike appeared on the bookie's roof after his stag night. And the mystery of the burned-out Mini in the bucket of the JCB. But this was a first, an upturned Escort amongst the daisies. Betty's neighbour Angela took some snaps with her Polaroid and passed them around the crowd, and a man from across the road arrived with his camcorder and proceeded to film the event. Betty rested one hand against the car and smiled like a big-game hunter, but when the cameraman panned across the crowd, and she realized that she was out of shot, she continued her narrative.

'Well, as soon as I recovered my senses I rushed outside to see what had happened. The wheels were still spinning and the windscreen was smashed and I could see these two lads inside, wearing balaclavas. They were moaning and that but I didn't know how bad they were injured. I didn't care either. I was bloody furious when I saw what they'd done to the lawn. I rushed into the garage and fetched the spade, and just as I got back, one of them was trying to crawl out through the windscreen. I gave him such a wallop that I knocked him spark out and he was lying there, half in, half out of the car.' She pointed to the spot and everybody scrutinized the grass for bloody evidence.

'The other one daren't move when he saw what had happened to his mate. It's a good job an' all. I was in such a temper, I'd have killed him. "You're not so bloody brave now are you?" I shouted at him. Then I gave the windscreen a smack with the spade and showered him with broken glass. He just lay there, blubbering like a bairn. It's a good job George wasn't here or I'd have been phoning for a hearse instead of an ambulance.'

8

With the story completed, people began to drift away. By the time the incident had been recycled across the estate and reached the local pubs that evening, Betty would have captured a couple of serial killers single-handed.

Eddie tried to close one of the car doors but it fell open like a broken wing.

'Do you want me to help you clean up or anything?'

'No, thanks. I might as well wait until they've towed the car away first.'

She started to gather the snapped privet twigs.

'God knows what George'll say when he sees this lot. You know how keen he is on his garden.'

'How much longer has he to do?'

'Three months. I should be able to get it sorted out by the time he gets out.'

She crouched down and tugged at the exposed privet roots.

'I don't know what they'll do about the hedge though. When that bloke ran amok with that flamethrower up at Summerfield, the council only put new fences up to replace the hedges he burned down. I mean, a hedge gives you a bit of privacy, doesn't it?'

Eddie nodded, admiring her legs as her short skirt worked up over her thighs.

'I was going to come to the cemetery, you know to pay my respects. I'd just got changed and then this lot happened,' standing up and indicating the wreckage.

Eddie looked at her T-shirt with the legend Nice Ones roller-coasting across the front, and wondered what she would have worn to a wedding.

'I was on my way to my mother's.'

9

He hesitated, realizing that he had no idea why he had come. After the farce of the vicar's mobile phone, followed by the flare-up with Pearl, he had instinctively set off for his mother's house like a hurt child running home.

Betty gently squeezed his arm.

'She had a hard time, your mother. What with Jack being like he was.'

Eddie admired her chunky diamond ring, set off against the dark material of his jacket sleeve, and wondered if it was part of the haul that George had been sent down for.

'I was just going to pick something up.'

'Do you need any help?'

Eddie imagined them fucking on his mother's bed with the curtains drawn. He was ashamed of his profane thoughts but he still got an erection. He felt Betty tighten her grip.

'I've got some beer in the house, if you'd like to drown your sorrows.'

Eddie could see them stretched out on the sofa with the racing turned down on the television. Then he saw Betty's husband, George, knocking on his door, with two of his accomplices in three months' time and, fearless as Eddie was, he changed his mind.

'No, thanks. I'd better be going. They'll wonder where I am.'

He stepped back through the broken hedge on to the pavement. Betty tried to follow him, but her high heels stuck in the lawn and she stumbled out of her shoes. When Eddie saw her standing there in her bare feet, he had second thoughts about going in for a drink. He could see her bare-footed on the hearthrug, unzipping her skirt. Betty stepped back into her shoes and tiptoed across the pavement.

'I'm going across to Kevin's house to look at the video of the crash. He think's he's Steven Spielberg, with that camera.'

She crossed the road and walked up the path. When she reached the house, she stopped and pointed to the name plate beside the front door.

'Look at this.'

'I can't read it from here.'

'Hollywood!'

Betty posed starlet-like, hand on hip, with pointed toe, then disappeared round the back of the house. A dog barked and Eddie laughed when he heard Betty shout, 'Lassie! Shut up!' I bet he's got a cat called Tom, Eddie thought, as he opened his mother's front gate. The neighbours, hearing the click of the latch and glancing through their windows, would have been puzzled to see Eddie laughing to himself and shaking his head. Must have been drowning his sorrows would have been the only logical explanation they could have come up with.

Eddie unlocked the back door and walked through the kitchen into the living room. The curtains were drawn and the room was gloomy and silent and the smell of cheap scent and cigarette smoke from the mourners hung sickeningly in the stale air. As Eddie pushed back the curtains to open the window, he noticed the goldfish bowl on the window-sill. The water was green and the fish was gulping for air, its top lip skimming the surface like a periscope.

'Poor little bugger,' Eddie said, carrying the bowl through to the kitchen. He filled the washing-up bowl with cold water, then pulled a face as he carefully poured the stinking green water down the sink. The fish struggled against the pull. Then, as it splashed in the shallows, Eddie tipped the bowl and the fish was carried over the lip on a little waterfall. He felt relieved for it as he watched it exploring its new surroundings. The water looked so cool and tempting that he could have dived in himself and kept the fish company.

Eddie left the kitchen and went upstairs. He looked into his old bedroom, the smallest of the three, then into his sisters' room, with its cosy double bed. The only clues to the previous occupants were the candlewick bedspreads: a blue one covering Eddie's bed and a pink one on the girls'. The walls had been repapered with sober patterns, and unwanted Christmas presents and chipped ornaments littered the surface of the melamine chests and dressing-table in Brenda and Carol's room. They were anonymous, depressing places and reminded Eddie of the cheap boarding houses he had stayed in when he worked away from home on short-term labouring jobs.

He was anxious to leave now; the house revived too many unhappy memories. He wanted to lock the door behind him and never return. But first, there was something he had to find out. He crossed the landing and entered his mother's room. If she had kept it, it would be here, in the wardrobe, in one of the bags of old clothes she refused to throw away simply because they had gone out of fashion. 'It'll come in for something,' she would say, rescuing a discarded jacket or sweater from the dustbin.

Eddie could have cried when he opened the wardrobe doors and saw the paucity of his mother's garments spread out on the rail. There were a few shabby dresses and skirts and incongruously, an expensive coat still wrapped in polythene, which Eddie had bought her after a good win on the horses.

'I'm saving it for a special occasion,' she replied when he asked her why she never wore it. Perhaps we should have buried her in it, Eddie thought, as he pushed her clothes to the end of the rail. You don't get a more special occasion than that.

There was no need to open most of the bags; he could tell by their weight and texture through the paper that they didn't contain what he was looking for. He started to feel foolish, then angry with himself. What the hell was he doing here, rummaging through his mother's wardrobe, when everybody else was at the wake? They would be asking about him now, wondering where he was. He glanced round to make sure that nobody had come to find him and was watching from the doorway. And what if he did find it? So what? What was he trying to prove? He wasn't sure. It was a waste of time anyway; even his mother wouldn't have kept it all this time. He quickly pulled out the remaining bags, eager to finish the search and get out of the house. Then he saw it, squashed and bulging in the corner, the original white bag, with the tailor's name across it. Eddie's heart thumped as he picked it up. He tried to ward off hope and avoid disappointment, but after the search and unexpected discovery, if it wasn't what he thought it was, the bag and its deceitful contents would go straight through the window.

Holding his breath, he pulled open the bag and looked in.

'Yes!'

It was the jubilant cry of a child receiving exactly what he wanted at Christmas. Eddie tipped out the contents on to the bed. It was a suit. A crimson Teddy-boy suit, the same colour as the stem of fireweed which he had placed on Jet's grave. He shook the crumpled drainpipes to straighten them out, and when he held them against his legs in front of the mirror on the wardrobe door, it all came back, the day he had gone to collect it from the tailor's with Jet . . . Easing up the trousers in the curtained booth, then stepping back into the shop, where the assistant, dark-suited, with his tape round his neck, called him 'sir', as he helped him on with the jacket. And, oh! that first glorious sight of himself in the mirror, with Jet wearing a similar suit in midnight blue, grinning approvingly behind him.

He had saved up for months, working overtime and staying in during the week to save money, but now, as Jet moved away and he had the mirror to himself, he knew that the sacrifices had been worth it. It was a dream suit. The best suit ever made. If there had been a suit Olympics, it would have won gold. Jet joined him at the mirror again and Eddie was so delighted with himself, that he put his arm round his pal's shoulders and they laughed uproariously at their outrageous reflections.

Eddie kept his new suit on, and as they paraded up and down the High Street, with people nudging each other and staring, he felt like Elvis Presley, like Rocky Marciano, like James Dean all rolled into one. Handsome Jet and tough Eddie, the first Teddy boys in town.

Jet had always been a trend-setter. He was the first boy to have a D A haircut. He walked into Tommy Ward's barber shop with a side parting, explained what he wanted, and twenty minutes later he looked like a teenage heart-throb with his new swept-back style. When Eddie took his turn in the chair and Tommy asked him what he wanted, he pointed at Jet and said, 'Cut it like his.' Tommy looked down at

Eddie's lank mop and shook his head doubtfully. But he accepted the challenge, and after sterling work with the dryer and lashings of Brylcreem, he managed to tame Eddie's hair into place, complete with a Tony Curtis-style quiff.

Eddie was trying to squeeze into the trousers of his Teddy-boy suit. First he had tried standing up, but the legs were too narrow and he kept overbalancing. So now he was sitting on his mother's bed trying to ease the crumpled material over his feet. He bent over, but his stomach got in the way, so he lay on his back with his legs in the air, blaming the trousers for having shrunk. So what if he had filled out a bit over the years? It was only natural at his age. But he couldn't understand why his legs had put on weight too. It was muscle, not fat, he concluded. Built up pounding the streets looking for work.

He finally gave up the struggle with the trousers. They were so tight that, when he yanked them off, his socks peeled off with them. He put his dark suit trousers back on then tried on the red drape jacket. It was tight across the shoulders and the link button wouldn't fasten, but when he looked at himself in the wardrobe mirror, he experienced the same thrill as when he had tried it on in the shop. He smoothed his fingers down the rolled collar, slipped his hands into the half-moon pockets, neatly finished with stitched arrow heads at each end, then measured the length with his arms by his side. It was longer than he'd thought. It stretched down past his finger tips, almost to his knees. His memory completed the outfit with trousers and shoes, then he walked away from the wardrobe and watched himself walk back across the room.

'Bloody hell, what times we had, eh kid?' As if Jet was standing behind him at the mirror. Guiltily, he made a quick search of his mother's dressing-table to see if she had saved any of his old Slim Jim ties. The bottom drawer was stiff and, as he yanked it open, the jerky movement disturbed a silky underskirt, which slid across the shiny cover of a book concealed underneath it. The last four letters of the title, HOTS, extended suggestively from the hem of the slip, the rest of the title hidden beneath the filigree.

Eddie stared at it. His unexpected discovery released painful childhood memories and he tried to kick the drawer shut. But it jammed, and when he bent down he couldn't resist the temptation and he reached inside and picked up the book, revealing the full title on the cover: SNAPSHOTS. He sat on the bed and worked it out. It was hard to believe, but it was over thirty years since the last time he had seen it.

Jack used to sit on the sofa by the fire with Brenda and Carol on either side of him and Eddie hovering around the back, trying to glimpse the photographs between their heads. He wanted to be on the sofa too, pointing and asking questions about the war in Burma, where Jack had spent four years fighting the Japanese. He hated Jack so much for excluding him that he wished he had been captured and died like the soldiers building the Burma railway.

Eddie slowly turned the pages and studied the photographs of Jack and his comrades sitting around camp fires in jungle clearings, dressed in baggy shorts and wide-brimmed hats. There were snaps of mules heavily loaded with supplies struggling up narrow mountain tracks, and a photograph of a parachute drop of ammunition and rations over the jungle.

Eddie remembered Jack trying not to laugh when he recalled the story of one unfortunate soldier being killed when he was hit by a sack load of new boots crashing through the trees. He also remembered Jack staring into the fire with his hands round his mug complaining bitterly that he had walked twice as far looking for a job since he had returned home, as he had trudging through Burma. When he was in this mood, everybody kept out of his way.

Eddie turned the last page and was just about to close the album, when he noticed underneath the loose collection of holiday snaps and school portraits a bundle of crinkly airmail letters tied with a blue ribbon. They were addressed to his mother in Jack's handwriting and bore the official army stamp. He flicked the corners, turned them over, replaced them in the album, then took them out again. He fiddled with the ribbon and tried to ease it over the corner of the bundle like a shoulder strap, as if gaining access without untying the knot was somehow less intrusive. But in the end he couldn't resist it, and his hands shook guiltily as he picked at the knot.

Eddie had booked the function room in his local, the Greyhound, for his mother's funeral tea. The landlord had opened the bar for the occasion and the landlady had provided a spread of cold meats and sandwiches. By the time Eddie arrived, the atmosphere had turned festive. Small children ran around as if it was a party, while their mothers, laughing and weeping in turn, spoke fondly of Eddie's mother and caught up on family news. The men had taken off their jackets and, as they stood in groups at the bar, uniformly dressed in dark trousers and white shirts, they looked like a male voice choir or a brass band relaxing after a performance.

When Eddie walked in, wearing his crimson Teddy-boy jacket and carrying his mother's goldfish in a polythene sandwich bag, everybody went quiet and two of Eddie's granddaughters, who had sneaked under the tables with a stolen bowl of crisps, suddenly appeared from under the white cloths to see where everybody had gone. Eddie paused in the doorway and looked round. The adults looked away, embarrassed, but the children were more interested in the goldfish than Eddie's jacket.

'What's up with you all?' Eddie said, walking across to the bar. 'Anybody'd think it was a funeral.'

There was shocked laughter at his irreverence, but it broke the tension and the room became noisy again. Eddie handed the sandwich bag over the bar to the landlord.

'Here. Put that in something for me, will you, Dean?'

The landlord poured the goldfish into a pint glass, then topped it up from a jug of water on the bar. Eddie watched it struggling against the deluge like a salmon under a waterfall.

'Hey up, steady on! Or we'll have another death on our hands, if we're not careful.'

They watched the water settle, then the landlord placed the glass on a shelf behind the bar and the goldfish nosed up to its reflection in the mirror.

'I've had all sorts in this pub: dogs, cats, ferrets, even a monkey once. But it's the first time anybody's brought a pet goldfish in,' the landlord said, pulling Eddie a pint.

'It's my mother's.' As if this explained everything.

'Are you taking it on a fancy dress parade?'

Eddie stared at him, mystified. He thought he was talking about the goldfish.

'What do you mean?'

'Your outfit.'

Eddie looked down at himself. He appeared to have no idea how absurd he looked, wearing a Teddy-boy jacket with crumpled suit trousers.

'Why, what's wrong with it?'

The landlord didn't like his tone of voice and waved away his money.

'It's on the house. For your mother. She was a nice lady. I'm sure you'll all miss her.'

Eddie nodded tearfully and felt in his pockets for his handkerchief, but he had left it in his suit jacket in his mother's bedroom. The landlord handed him a serviette from behind the bar, and Eddie was blowing his nose, when Pearl approached, hissing and tutting and shaking her head.

'Where've you been? Just look at you! Honestly!'

Eddie handed her the damp serviette and Pearl stuffed it into her handbag. The snap of the closing clasp emphasized her disapproval.

'I walked down to my mother's. You know, Memory Lane and all that.'

Pearl leaned into him and smelled his breath.

'You've been drinking!'

Eddie pointed to his pint on the bar.

'You don't have to be Sherlock Holmes to work that out.'

'I don't mean that. I mean whisky. I can smell it on your breath.'

Eddie picked up the glass and started to drink. The landlord was pulling a second pint before Eddie had finished his first.

'I'm waiting, Eddie. I want to know where you've been.'

She was trying to keep her voice down and look calm, but it was obvious from her expression that she wasn't telling him a joke. Eddie placed the empty glass on the bar.

'I've told you. I went to my mother's.'

'What, all this time?' tapping her watch face. 'And leaving everything to me and your Brenda and Carol. She was your mother as well, you know.'

Eddie watched the white foam streaming down the side of the empty glass.

'I was reading.'

That shut her up. Pearl thought that she had heard every conceivable excuse from him for being late, but this was a new one, the daddy of them all. It was even more implausible than his story about chasing the escaped llama from the circus on his way home from the pub.

'Reading? Reading what?'

'Oh, you know . . . Wartime stuff. Jack's letters and that. I just wanted a bit of time on my own, that's all. Have a last look round . . .'

Pearl nodded, softening. She was starting to believe him when she smelled his breath again.

'You're lying to me Eddie. You've been in a pub. You've called in at the Cross Keys on your way here.'

'I haven't. Honest! There was a drop of whisky left in the sideboard so I finished it before the vultures moved in.'

'What vultures? Who do you mean?'

Eddie nodded over Pearl's shoulder towards his elder sister, Brenda, who was disdainfully surveying the refreshments on the side table.

'Our Brenda, for one. She'd have taken it even though she doesn't drink.'

'Ssh! She'll hear you!'

Pearl's whispered warning was so loud that Brenda paused and glanced round as she picked up a vol-au-vent.

'I don't care if she does.'

'But what about this, Eddie?' Pearl touched his jacket. 'Have you any idea what you look like?'

Eddie turned round and tried to look at his reflection in the mirror behind the bar, but the optics and rows of bottles on the shelves only allowed him a fragmented view of himself.

'I got a bit carried away, I suppose. You know, being in the house on my own. All the memories came flooding back.'

Eddie breathed in deeply and fastened the button of his jacket.

'They don't make 'em like this any more.'

Pearl shook her head and laughed.

'Honestly, Eddie. You're like a big kid sometimes.'

'Do you remember it?'

Pearl stroked the satin lapels.

'Of course I remember it. You and Jet strutting around town in your Teddy-boy suits as if you owned the place.'

'We did own it! There was nobody to touch us, me and Jet!'

He glanced round, challenging anybody to deny it, but nobody met his bloodshot glare. Then he heard a whisper:

'Jet and the Jailbirds.'

The voice came from behind him: a ghostly reminder from the distant past. Eddie turned pale and gripped the bar rail. He felt a hand on his arm. When he braced himself and turned round, his younger sister Carol was grinning at him. Eddie shrugged her off, angrily.

'You silly bugger!'

Carol stared at him, bemused.

'What do you mean?'

'You nearly gave me a heart attack, sneaking up on me like that.'

He unbuttoned his jacket and took deep breaths.

'I didn't sneak up on you. I heard you mention Jet, that's all. I meant it as a joke.'

Eddie realized that he had hurt Carol's feelings and gave her a hug.

'Sorry about that. You made me jump. Anyway, how can you remember that?'

'Remember what?' Wincing as she recovered from his embrace.

'Jet and the Jailbirds.'

'I was there.'

'Where?'

'In the house. That night you were talking about getting a band together. You and Jet and Frankie Mellor.'

Eddie stared at the dimple in Carol's chin and remembered how Jet used to tease her with the Rosemary Clooney hit record of the time . . . *On the baby's bottom or the baby's knee/Where will the baby's dimple be?*

He started to laugh.

'That's right! And our Brenda was trying to do her homework.'

And Frankie was sitting across the table from her, drumming on the sugar basin with two knives. Eddie was lying on the sofa, strumming on his cricket bat, and Jet was standing on the hearthrug, using a sweeping brush as a mike. This was the proposed line-up: vocalist, guitar and drums. All they needed now were some instruments and a name for the band. Jet started them off.

'Jet and the Jays?'

Then Eddie and Frankie joined in.

'Jet and the Jayhawks?'

'What's a jayhawk?'

'An American bird.'

'I bet it's a funny-looking bugger, a cross between a jay and a hawk.'

Jet tried again.

'Jet and the Janitors?'

'What's a janitor?'

'An American caretaker.'

'Remember old Rodgers the school caretaker, with all them copies of *Razzle* in his overalls?'

'Dirty bastard.'

They all laughed, and Brenda blushed as red as the map of the British empire in the atlas in front of her. Frankie leaned across the table and played a drum solo on a jar of jam.

'Jet and the Jam?'

'Jet and the Jelly!' Eddie added, shaking all over. They turned giddy then, firing off silly names and gasping and crying with laughter.

'The Jigsaws! The Jumps! The Jockstraps!'

The last suggestion doubled them up and Jet fell to his knees, weeping into his brush-handle mike, like Johnnie Ray. Amidst all the jollity, Frankie attempted a spot of footsie under the table with Brenda. But when she kicked him on the shin, he retired to an armchair sulking and picked up a *Superman* comic.

'Jet and the Jailbirds,' he said a few minutes later, when

Eddie and Jet had run out of ideas and were already talking about splitting up the band. They looked round at him. Frankie held up the comic and read out a caption in an American accent.

'"Jailbirds run riot in Gotham City!"'

Eddie and Jet stared at each other. There was no need to say anything. Jet and the Jailbirds. That was it! They saw it up in lights. They were millionaires already. They owned mansions and limousines. They saw their pictures in the papers fighting off hordes of screaming girls. *Roll over Beethoven/Tell Tchaikovsky the news . . .*

Carol finished her mini sausage roll and placed the paper plate on the bar.

'What happened to Frankie? Didn't he go abroad somewhere?'

Eddie ordered another pint and drinks for Carol and Pearl.

'Yeah. He emigrated to Australia with his mother and dad.' He started to laugh. 'He got put away for a robbery in Perth.'

In spite of herself, Carol began to laugh too.

'It's not funny really.'

'I know. Poor old Frankie. He became a real jailbird. The only one of us who made it.'

'Perhaps he started a band in jail . . . Frankie and the Felons.'

'Frankie and the Footpads,' Pearl suggested.

'What's a footpad?' Carol asked.

They were still laughing and trying to think up names for Frankie's band when Brenda approached, pumped up with righteous indignation.

'Honestly! I think it's disgusting. Haven't you got any respect?'

Eddie turned round and Brenda stepped back from his beery breath.

'What do you mean?'

'It's my mother's funeral, for God's sake, and you're treating the whole thing as a joke!'

Brenda paused, expecting a response, but Eddie just stared at her. If she had been a man, she would have known instinctively that she had said enough. She looked to Pearl and Carol for support but they were looking elsewhere. She turned back to Eddie.

'You disappear from the cemetery before the service is over. Then you turn up here drunk, dressed like a, like a . . .' She shuffled her pack of insults then dealt the ace. 'Like a lout! It's an insult to my mother. It's disrespectful.'

She was trying to keep her voice down to avoid a scene, but her words escaped in a hiss like steam from a pressure cooker. Eddie waited for her to finish, then picked up his fresh pint from the bar and began to drink, each swallow metered by his bobbing Adam's apple. Brenda watched in disgust, her head unconsciously tilting backwards as he drained his glass, until finally she found herself staring at the plastic chandelier in the middle of the ceiling. Eddie smacked his empty glass on to the bar and Brenda ricked her neck when she jerked down her head, and the pain grew worse when Eddie grinned at her and ordered another pint.

'You're disgusting,' she said, massaging the back of her neck.

'Whatever I am, it's better than being a snob and bloody hypocrite like you.'

Brenda opened her mouth to object, but Eddie stopped her with a pointed finger.

'You've had your say. It's my turn now.'

Brenda knew better than to object. Unless she was prepared for a public row.

'Don't you dare accuse me of disrespect. I thought the world of my mother. She had a hard life one way or another, but she did her best for us. All three of us.'

Carol nodded and dabbed her eyes with her serviette, darkening the pale blue to navy.

'I left the cemetery because I was disgusted at what happened at the grave side. It turned her burial into a farce. I couldn't stand it. I didn't want to remember her leaving us like that. OK, perhaps it is going too far wearing this jacket, but I was upset. I don't know why I went really, trying to bring back old times, I suppose . . . Then I found my old Teddy-boy suit in the wardrobe.' He looked down at himself and laughed. 'I must have looked a real bobby-dazzler.' He measured the length of the jacket again and shook his head. 'I still can't believe it.'

Carol sipped her brandy and Coke and looked mischievously at Brenda.

'We were talking about Jet. Can you remember him?'

Brenda furrowed her brow theatrically.

'Jeff Jones. What about him?'

'How all the girls fancied him.'

'I didn't fancy him.'

Carol laughed.

'Of course you did! You used to wait for him and follow him home after school.'

'*I did not!*'

She made it sound as if she had been accused of murder.

'Yes, you did! Everybody liked Jet, didn't they Pearl?'

Carol continued her eulogy without waiting for an answer, and Eddie was the only one who noticed that Pearl was blushing.

'He was the first boy in town to wear a Teddy-boy suit.'

And I was the second, Eddie thought.

'And his hair.' She sculptured the proud plume above her head. 'It was black and shiny and swept back, like this.'

Eddie hoped that she would remember his hairstyle too, but he was disappointed for the second time, as Carol closed her eyes and feigned a teenage swoon.

'Oh, he sends me,' she sighed, falling into Pearl's arms.

Pearl laughed, but she was blinking away tears and Eddie felt jealous at the thought of her grieving over Jet. Brenda looked as if she was sucking a lemon as she watched Carol's performance.

'Jeff Jones. He was as common as muck.'

Carol straightened up and brushed down her dress with her hand.

'You didn't think that when you asked me to deliver that love letter.'

'I did nothing of the kind!'

Eddie picked up Carol's mischief and ran with it.

'Yes, you did. He showed it to me. "Darling Jeff" . . .' He raised his hand and appeared to be reading his palm. '"I love you from the bottom of my heart, and when I go to bed I can't go to sleep for thinking about you."' He paused, realizing that it sounded like the letters he used to compose to Pearl but never had the courage to send. Eddie stared at

27

his palm, unable to continue, as if the letter had been written in disappearing ink.

'You're a liar!'

He didn't hear her. He was back in the Cats Eyes, where they had first met.

'I never wrote anything of the kind.'

Eddie was jerked back to the present, face to face with his vengeful sister.

'You're making it all up. It's a lie.'

'No, it's not. We passed it round the lads at work and had a good laugh.'

Pearl and Carol were trying hard to suppress their laughter. They knew he was making it up, but they were enjoying Brenda's discomfort so much that they had no intention of stopping him.

'Yes, that's the sort of dirty trick you'd do.'

'No. That's the sort of dirty trick *you*'d do, you vicious cow.'

He emphasized the accusation with a jabbing finger. If it had connected, it would have damaged her collar bone. Brenda stepped back in alarm.

'Don't you dare threaten me, you hooligan!'

'Why, what are you going to do, fetch your husband to sort me out?'

'You're disgusting.'

'Is that why he's not here, because you think I'll show you up?'

'No, it's not . . .' She faltered, her lips marking time as she scrambled for an excuse.'

'He's working.'

Eddie laughed.

'That's what you think. I bet he's gone to see a stripper with his mates.'

Pearl and Carol could contain themselves no longer. The thought of that mild little man, red-faced and roaring drunk, yelling 'Ger 'em off!' was too much for them and they started to laugh.

Brenda was outraged at their complicity.

'At least I've still got a husband,' she said, glaring at Carol.

Carol glared back and Pearl gripped her arm just in case she was tempted to use it.

'What happened between me and Sean has nothing to do with you, so just keep your nose out. And our Eddie's right, you are ashamed of us. You're nothing but a snob.'

But the gibe about her divorce had upset her and her retaliation tailed off in tears. Eddie put his arm round her and gave her a cuddle.

'Who do you think you are anyway, turning your nose up at everybody? It hardly makes you Brain of Britain, going to college and doing cookery. Bloody hell, my mother was one of the best cooks there was, and she didn't go any-where.'

'It wasn't cookery. It was Domestic Science.'

'And it was Home Economics when our Jane was at school. They're all the same thing with jazzed-up names. God knows how you passed, 'cause you couldn't boil a bloody egg when you lived at home.'

Carol was laughing again. Her tears and mascara had stained Eddie's jacket.

'You only came up to make sure that me and Carol didn't divide all my mother's stuff between us.'

'That's a lie!'

'I bet you've been round the house already, sniffing out what you can take home.'

'There's nothing worth taking, I can assure you!'

Eddie grinned.

'What did I say?'

Brenda was furious at being caught out. She pointed at Eddie's jacket.

'It looks as if you've got your share, anyway.'

'My share? This?' He gazed down at himself, slowly shaking his head. 'My old suit jacket.' He looked up at Brenda.

'Why, do you want it?'

'Don't be ridiculous.'

'Here, you can have it.'

He took off his jacket and held it out by the collar.

'Go on, take it. Take everything. Perhaps your husband can wear it to the office. There's a pair of trousers back at the house that might fit him as well.'

Brenda blushed. People were starting to look.

'You're making an exhibition of yourself.'

'Oh, I nearly forgot.' Eddie felt in his jacket pocket and produced an old photograph from the family album. 'You might as well have this photo of my mother and dad while you're at it.'

Brenda stepped forward and smacked away the photograph.

'He wasn't your dad! Not your real dad anyway!'

She shouted so loud that the room went quiet. Nobody moved. Anything could happen now. Eddie stared at the photograph then carefully slid it back into his pocket.

'No, he wasn't my real dad. But he was the only one I'd got.'

Carol handed her glass to Pearl, then slapped Brenda so hard across the face that her glasses flew off and skidded across the floor.

Eddie and Pearl lay with their backs to each other, listening to the music from next door. It was all bass and no melody, thud-thud-thud-thud throbbing through the wall. Eddie started to get out of bed. Pearl turned her head towards him.

'Where you going?'

'Where do you think?'

'Leave it, Eddie. You know what he's like.'

'Yeah, and he'll know what it's like if he doesn't turn it down.'

Pearl gripped his vest to restrain him.

'Please, Eddie. I think we've had enough trouble for one day.'

Eddie paused then turned over and cuddled up to Pearl's back.

'It wasn't my fault what happened, you know.'

She ignored him and tried to wipe out the shaming embarrassment of the funeral by recalling happier family occasions, when the children were small. Jane as the Virgin Mary in the primary school nativity play, and Danny riding a donkey in his cowboy outfit on the beach at Scarborough . . .

'You blame me for what happened, don't you?'

Thud-thud-thud-thud.

'Go to sleep, Eddie.'

'I was upset.'

'You were drunk.'

'It was our Brenda's fault.'

'You egged her on.'

'She'll be blubbing to Ralph now, back in Burton.'

'Bedford.'

'Who cares? She's not worth arguing about.'

Pearl lay stiffly beside him and did not reply. Eddie thought about Betty and replayed the scene after the car crash on her lawn . . . She invited him into the house and this time he accepted. He sat down on the sofa and Betty gave him a can of lager. After a couple more she put on a sexy video and cuddled up beside him . . .

Pearl felt Eddie stirring against her buttocks. She removed his hand from her breasts and nudged him away.

'What's the matter?'

'I've got to go to work in the morning.'

'Yeah, I wish I was going with you.'

He reached up and pulled the light cord above the padded headboard. Pearl squinted in the sudden light then yanked the sheet over her head.

'Eddie! What you doing?'

He leaned across to the bedside table for his cigarettes and matches and lit up.

'You'll be setting the bed on fire.'

Eddie anticipated Pearl's warning and accompanied her in silent mockery behind her back. He pulled the light switch then leaned back against the headboard in the darkness.

Two drunks passed by, roaring gibberish at each other. Eddie was an expert in the language, but the only word he could understand was 'pal'. It was 'pal' this and 'pal' that. They were great pals. They'll be fighting before they get to the end of the street, Eddie thought, listening to a police-car siren in the distance. Or was it an ambulance? Or the fire brigade? A dog started barking nearby, a vicious, teeth-bared, snarling bark. Eddie hoped that it wasn't barking at the two drunks, but he couldn't help grinning at the thought of them addressing it as 'pal' as they tried to placate it. And all the time the thud of the bass beat through the wall. Selfish bastard. Didn't he sleep? Footsteps approaching down the street: somebody running fast. Eddie was about to get up and look out of the window, but by the time he had stubbed out his cigarette, the footsteps had receded. He wondered if it was a burglar being pursued by the dog, and hoped for the bloke's sake that it wasn't next door's Rottweiler.

'Poor bugger,' Eddie said, laughing, as he imagined the dog at the burglar's throat.

'What?' Pearl raised her head from the pillow.

'Did you hear that lad running past?'

'For God's sake, Eddie! I was asleep!'

She turned over, dragging the duvet with her. Eddie lit another cigarette in the dark.

'It's Jet, isn't it?'

'What is? What are you on about now?'

'You, turning over. Avoiding me and that. It brought it all back, didn't it? In the cemetery. Then in the Greyhound, when we were talking about starting up a band and that. I could see it in your face.'

'All you could see was me being embarrassed at the scene you caused with your Brenda.'

'It's true though, isn't it?'

'Eddie, we've had this out a thousand times.'

Every time she spoke, she reared up slightly and looked over her shoulder at him even though it was dark.

'We've been married thirty-odd years. We've had two kids. We've got grandchildren. What more do you want, for God's sake?'

Before Eddie could reply, there was banging on the adjoining wall and a muffled voice from the other side.

'For fuck's sake, keep your voices down, will you? Some of us are trying to get some sleep!'

Is it a bird? No! Is it a plane? No! Is it the twister? No! It was Eddie cruising the estate in a 1955 crimson Cadillac convertible with the hood down. A convoy had built up behind him as he drove slowly down the middle of Attlee Drive. Vehicles approaching from the opposite direction had to edge up on to the pavement until the procession passed by. Eddie sat proudly at the wheel, wearing a vest and wraparound shades, waving royally and sounding the horn at friends and lookers-on. Children trotted beside the car, begging for a ride. Eddie warned them not to touch the paintwork or he would chop their fucking fingers off. A pack of dogs lost interest in a bitch on heat and barked wildly at the approaching monster with its bulging eyes and glittering chrome teeth. Eddie gave them a long burst of the horn and they ran off with their tails between their legs and the whites of their eyes showing as they looked back. The mounted dog followed on behind, pushing the bitch before him, like a man wheeling a barrow.

The news had spread before him and the regulars at the Greyhound were out on the forecourt, drinks in hand, waiting as he approached the pub. When he stopped, they surrounded him, laughing and cheering, admiring the car and bombarding him with facetious questions. Whose was it? Where had he nicked it from? Had he won the pools? Eddie just grinned and warned them to be careful not to spill any beer on the leather. He revved the engine to clear the way, and when he saw them raise their glasses in the rear-view mirror, he felt like a conquering hero.

'This is the life!' he roared, slotting an Elvis tape into the player. 'This is definitely *the* fucking life!'

Eddie was singing along to 'King Creole', with one hand on the steering-wheel, the other acknowledging his fans, when he saw his son Danny at the top of a ladder, tiling a house roof. Danny had heard the music from streets away, but when the Cadillac came round the corner and he saw Eddie at the wheel, he nearly swallowed the tacks between his teeth. Eddie stopped in front of the house and grinned up at him.

'Fancy a spin?'

'Bloody hell! Where you got that from?'

'I found it in the street! Where do you think?'

'Whose is it?'

'It's mine!'

'Yeah? I didn't know you'd come up on the lottery!'

'Don't you start! Honest! I've just bought it.'

They were both shouting to make themselves heard over the Elvis tape. Danny unconsciously picked up the beat and made the ladder sway with a jerking knee, as he stared down at his father. He had always been a romancer, especially after a few beers. The careers he could have followed – if only . . . The celebrities he'd met – including Prince Charles, who had invited him to Buckingham Palace during a visit to the steelworks. The countries he'd visited. The countries he intended to visit in the future. But it was only make believe and easy to laugh off. But this was different. His old man, an old rocker with thinning, slicked-back hair was grinning up at him from a gleaming soft top, straight out of Hollywood.

Eddie pointed at the house.

'What's happened to the roof?'

'He's sold the slates and done a runner.'

Eddie blew the horn and started to laugh. He knew people who were so hard up that they had sold their lawns, but this was the first time he had heard of anybody selling his roof. He couldn't see for tears and he lit a cigarette to stop himself coughing.

'I'll see you later. Bring the kids round and I'll give them a ride.'

He drove away, leaving Danny amused but totally bewildered as to how his father had come by such a stunning motor. Eddie turned up the volume and, swaying in time to the beat, toured the estate, accompanying Elvis at the top of his voice: poetry in motion.

Pearl was shepherding the children across the road when she heard the music. It seemed to be coming from the direction of the park, and for a moment or two she thought that the fair had arrived. But as the sound grew louder and more focused, she realized that it was coming from an approaching vehicle. A group of children waiting outside the school gates were pointing excitedly down the line of traffic, but Pearl couldn't see what they were staring at because a bus was blocking her view. She beckoned to the children with her lollipop.

'Come on! We haven't got all day!'

The children hurried across the road. Pearl watched them safely to the other side, then called to the new gathering to stay where they were, before she left the middle of the road. Now that she was back on the pavement, she could identify the source of the music. It *had* to be that flashy, red American job with the white hood. The other cars didn't look strong enough to withstand the impact of 'Jailhouse Rock' at such volume.

Pearl started to tap the tip of her lollipop on the ground and sing along in her head. *Everybody in the old cell block/ Was dancing to the Jailhouse Rock* . . . She was back in the Cats Eyes, her flared skirt swirling around her waist as Eddie spun her round. God, how he could jive. You wouldn't think so, looking at him now, but he was slim in those days. You never put weight on in the rolling-mill with all that heat, he used to say. He was in total control: a push, a twirl, then briefly face to face again. And he was so quick and light on his feet. He would fall back on his hands and spring up again before she'd finished spinning. He jives like a nigger, the other boys used to sneer. Pearl closed her eyes for a moment and she could smell his Brylcreem as they danced to Elvis singing 'Jailhouse Rock'.

It's like the cars on the films I used to see at the Alhambra, Pearl thought, as she watched the Cadillac creep forward in the solid line of traffic, with courting couples necking in the back seat at a drive-in movie. When she arrived home and her mother asked her what the film was about, she had to make it up, because she had spent most of the time snogging on the back row with Jet.

Pearl walked out into the middle of the road and planted her lollipop in front of the Cadillac. She wanted to hold it there, to prolong the sweet memories for a few more precious seconds. She feigned indifference as the children passed in front of the wide bonnet, secretly trailing their fingers across the hot chrome grille. Pearl tried to look at the driver, but the hood was raised and the sun was reflecting off the windscreen. She wanted more children to appear through the school gates, to keep them crossing, to prevent the car and the memories from disappearing, but all the children had gone now and she turned reluctantly towards the pavement. She paused when 'Love Me Tender' followed 'Jailhouse Rock' on the tape. It was her favourite ballad and she was back in the Alhambra again with Jet's arm around her, his fingers tracing the lace trimming of her bra through her blouse. Elvis was serenading his sweetheart . . . *For you make my life complete/And I love you so*. Then Jet leaned across her and kissed her and she wanted to remain in the cosy darkness for ever.

Harsh sunlight and the blare of car horns destroyed her reverie. A line of traffic had built up behind the Cadillac and irate drivers were straining out of their windows to see what was causing the hold-up. Embarrassed and painfully exposed in the middle of the road, Pearl ducked her head to hide her blushes under the peak of her cap. But as she turned away, the music from the car grew louder, and when she looked back, the hood was folding back over the seats, followed by Eddie rising up behind the windscreen, singing a duet with Elvis. *Love me tender/Love me sweet*, he implored, arms outstretched over the car bonnet towards her. She stared at him. She was paralysed. She couldn't speak. She couldn't think . . . It couldn't be. And the car? It was a hoax. Wotsisname on the telly? A crowd had gathered on the pavements.

They didn't know what was happening either, but it was worth watching. One man said, 'They must be making a film.' 'What, with Eddie Brooks in it?' his wife replied. Eddie and Elvis finished their duet and Eddie blew kisses towards the audience. If Pearl's lollipop had been a shotgun, he would have been dead.

'Eddie! What do you think you're playing at?'

'*Riding along in my automobile/My baby beside me at the wheel*,' he sang with a convincing southern drawl. But in his grubby white vest, and sporting a two-day stubble, there was no way that he could have been mistaken for an American tourist, even though he was driving a Cadillac.

'Whose is it?'

'It's mine. Whose do you think it is?'

'Yours! Oh, my God!'

She feared the worst. Was that a police-car siren she could hear in the distance?

'Where's it from? Where've you got it from?'

The audience was growing all the time and a gang of youths, arriving late and unaware of what was happening, pushed through the crowd, hoping to see an accident. When they saw who it was, they started pointing in unison and chanting football-style:

'E-ddie! E-ddie! E-ddie!'

'Route 66,' Eddie said, giving his fans a wave.

'Route 66? What are you talking about?' Pearl was becoming increasingly irritated by Eddie's flippancy.

'*Get your kicks on Route 66*,' the driver of the Ford Fiesta behind Eddie sang, admiring the shark-like fins of the Cadillac. It could swallow my car whole, he thought.

Pearl tightened her grip on the pole.

'You'll be getting your kicks on this route unless you start talking sense.'

She leaned forward to see if she could catch the smell of drink on his breath. But it would have needed an epic session for any fumes to have travelled the length of that car bonnet.

'It's up on the industrial estate.'

'What is?'

'Route 66.'

Pearl shook her head, bemused.

'So what?'

'It's a classic-car dealer's. That's what it's called.'

Pearl stared at Eddie with growing disbelief as the consequences became clear.

'You haven't bought it, have you?'

'Of course I've bought it! What do you think I've done, nicked it?'

Pearl shook her head. No. It was a joke. It was one of his stupid jokes.

'Look at the number plate if you don't believe me.'

Pearl stepped back and looked down. The registration plate read:

EDDIE

Pearl put her hand to her mouth.

'Oh, my God!'

Eddie grinned.

'Do you like it?'

Like it? Like it! Pearl couldn't find words strong enough to describe what she felt about both Eddie and the car. She turned and strode towards the pavement, striking the ground with her lollipop stick.

'Pearl! Pearl! Where are you going? I've come to give you a lift home!'

He stared at the car company logo on the back of her uniform coat, willing her to turn round but she kept on walking.

Eddie was polishing the headlamps when Pearl arrived home. The car took up most of the drive, and she had to edge along the side of it to avoid stepping on the flower bed. Eddie looked up at her and smiled, but she ignored him and went straight into the house. When he heard the door slam he peered down the side of the car to make sure that she hadn't scratched the bodywork with her shopping bag.

The word had spread across the estate and onlookers gathered outside Eddie's house to admire his car and question him about it. How old was it? Where did it come from? How fast did it go? How much did it cost? (Mind your own fucking business.) The fluctuating audience gave Eddie the opportunity to romance about the car's history. According to him, it had been owned by gangsters, film stars and pop stars. It has been specially shipped over for him from New York, Hollywood and Memphis, Tennessee. Elvis had owned it. President Kennedy had been shot in it, and it was the car that James Dean had crashed in on that fateful day in 1955. Eddie looked at his watch. He was running out of stories and he couldn't polish the car for ever. He was going to have to go in and face Pearl sometime. He worked it out . . . She set off for the White Hart about quarter to seven, so, if he went in at twenty to, there would be no time for an argument. He shook the tin of metal polish and began to whistle 'Wooden Heart'.

He was whistling 'Burning Love' when he sidled into the house twenty minutes later. Pearl, wearing her barmaid's uniform of black skirt and white blouse, was standing at the overmantel mirror, applying her lipstick. When she saw Eddie through the glass, she gave him a look of burning hate. He walked up behind her and put his arms around her.

'I like you in that outfit. You look dead sexy.'

It didn't work. She shrugged him off and replaced her lipstick in her make-up bag.

'You can take it back.'

'What?'

'That car. Get rid of it.'

'You what? I've only just bought it.'

'That's your problem.'

'I can't just take it back like that.'

'I'm not arguing with you, Eddie. I don't want it. We can't afford it. Just take it away.'

She checked her appearance in the mirror then picked up her handbag from the settee.

'I'll see you later.'

'I'll give you a lift, if you like.'

'No, thanks.'

'Go on.' He grinned and tried to put his arm around her. 'You'll feel like the Queen when you get in.'

Pearl twisted away from him and held up her hand as if she was stopping traffic.

'I don't want anything to do with it. I don't want a row, Eddie. I just want to come home from work tomorrow and find it gone. O K?'

She turned her back on him and left the house. Eddie hurried across to the window, hoping that he still might win her over by offering her a lift home when she had finished work. But when he saw her expression as she sidestepped past the car, trying not to touch it, he changed his mind and hoped she would topple forward on to the rose bushes. He was so angry that he nearly put his fist through the window, but he calmed himself by feeding his mother's goldfish, which was gulping up at him from its bowl on the window-sill.

Eddie was watching a late-night thriller on television when Pearl arrived home from the White Hart at midnight. She ignored him and went straight to bed. He was asleep when she got up at half past five the following morning to go office cleaning, and he was still in bed when she rushed in and rushed out wearing her white coat and peaked cap for her morning shift at the primary school. The window rattling slamming of the kitchen door warned Eddie that it was time to get up. He opened the curtains slightly and peered down. Pearl was traversing the drive with her back to the car like someone on a mountain ledge. Eddie wondered if he could placate her by widening the drive or placing a few stepping stones on the border. But he knew that tinkering with the garden wasn't the answer; she would never be satisfied until the car was gone. He cursed himself for being so stupid. Eight pints with his mates and a reckless boast and look where it had landed him. Pearl was right, he was a fool. But even so, as he gazed down at the Cadillac, glistening in the morning sunlight, he was still glad that he had bought it. He was awe-struck by its presence. It cheered him up just looking at it. It had transformed the garden into a technicolor film set. The flowers were brighter, the birds sang louder. People smiled at the car as they passed by, and even the neighbour's brute of a dog was wagging its tail as it looked through the dividing fence. Eddie swished open the curtains and basked in its glory. That was *his* car down there. His wish granted. His dream come true. Even if it was only for a day.

As he sat on the sofa, watching *Cartoon Capers* on television, Eddie wondered how much money he would lose on the deal when he returned the car, a calculation made more complicated by the two grand's worth of dud notes which he had bought half price from the two young hustlers. And how was he going to explain it to Ronnie at Route 66? 'My wife says I can't keep it; I've to bring it back.' Popeye wouldn't stand for it, he thought, watching a battleship appear in his bicep after squeezing a can of spinach down his throat. He went hot with shame at the thought of it. One day. One fucking day! It was pathetic. The milometer had barely clocked up four miles. He'd be a laughing stock. He'd be headlines in the local paper. People would point and snigger behind his back. He would have to leave town like Road-runner – zoom! in a puff of dust.

Eddie went into the kitchen and opened the refrigerator door, but he had finished off all the beer before he went to bed. He took out a carton of milk, but he was so busy thinking about the merciless ribbing he would receive from his mates in the Greyhound that he tilted the carton too far and the milk gushed down his chin. His yell, as the cold liquid splashed on to his chest and took his breath away, aroused the dog in the adjoining house into a barking frenzy. Eddie ripped off his damp vest and hurled it at the wall, then walked into the living room and looked out of the front window at the Cadillac. He had to play for time somehow. Tell the nosy bastards that he'd taken it in for a service or something. He groaned at the prospect of all the questions he was about to face. He had toured the estate like a one-car cavalcade, waving and saluting down every street and avenue, every road and drive. He had even cruised around the old folks' bungalows to make sure that they enjoyed the spectacle too. Eddie shook his head, sadly. Yesterday he was King of the Road. Today it was back to Shanks's pony.

He decided to make one last journey before returning the car. He bought two bunches of flowers with a dud twenty, then drove to the cemetery with the hood and windows closed, trying not to attract attention. It was the first time he had visited his mother's grave since the funeral and he felt guilty when he saw the new granite vase which he presumed had been bought by one of his sisters. He apologized to his mother for not visiting before, but he had been too upset, and he promised to make up for his neglect by buying her a marble headstone with the money he received back for the car. He added a bunch of red carnations to the gladioli in the vase, then remained on his knees by the grave looking across at the Cadillac parked inside the gates.

'You'd have understood, wouldn't you?' he said, softly, one hand resting on the bare soil. 'You might have had a car like that yourself if things had turned out differently. Who knows what might have happened, eh? Still, it's all blood under the bridge now, as they say. It's no good thinking about it. It all happened a long time ago now. Anyway, I just thought I'd bring it to show you before I took it back.'

Eddie patted the raised earth then stood up and crossed the cemetery to Jet's grave. The milk bottle had fallen over but the stem of fireweed was still protruding from the neck.

The red flower had seeded to a wispy beard and when Eddie tipped it out of the bottle, the white tufts drifted away like parachutes caught in a breeze.

Eddie refilled the bottle with water from a vase on the next grave, then inserted a single red carnation into the neck. He arranged the rest of the bunch in a fan near the headstone, then smoothed out the chippings and plucked out fresh weeds.

'Well, kid, remember what we said?'

As Eddie looked across the cemetery, at his car, a cortège entered the gates. He could see the mourners staring out of the windows and turning their heads for a lingering, last look as they drove slowly by. He was embarrassed by its flamboyance and wished that he had parked it outside, but he wanted to share it with Jet too.

'Remember what we were going to do when we won the pools? We were going to buy a big American car and take off. Hit the road. No more work. Pick some birds up. Have a good time. Remember Cynthia Hill? How we were going to kidnap her and take her with us? She was a runner-up in Miss Butlin's at Skegness one year. Finished up marrying a bloke who worked in the offices at Maitland and Brooks. What a fucking waste. She had the best tits in England, did Cynthia.'

Eddie kept glancing up from the grave to the sky, as if uncertain of Jet's final resting place.

'Remember how we had it all worked out? And how we got fed up of waiting to hit the jackpot and decided to rob a bank instead? Fucking hell, Jet, what a time we were going to have. It was going to be a right adventure.'

He tried to blink back the tears, but they ran down his

cheeks and dripped tinnily on to the discarded foil wrapping from the carnations.

'Well, I've done it at last.' He wiped his eyes and blew his nose on to the grass. 'It's a bit late in the day, I know. Stupid really. Pearl's right, but, what the fuck, you've got to have a few treats in your life, and I haven't had many of them lately, I can tell you.' He gazed across the cemetery at the car, shaking his head regretfully. 'I wish you could see it, kid. It's fantastic. It's a 55 Cadillac Eldorado convertible, left-hand drive. It's bright red with chrome-trim shark fins and white-wall tyres. It's what we used to dream about. You'd love it.'

He looked at his watch and stood up, his knees cracking like tinder.

'Old age creeping on. At least you avoided that.'

He didn't want to spoil the reunion by telling Jet that he was returning the car after he had left the cemetery, and as he walked back between the gravestones, he tried to console himself with the thought that there was no point in keeping it if he had nobody to share it with.

Eddie showed his respect for the nearby funeral service by resisting the satisfying clunk as he closed the heavy car door. But when he turned the ignition key, the deep rumble of the engine was more seductive than the vicar's words, and bowed heads turned surreptitiously to watch the departing Cadillac. He glanced up at the stone angels mounted on the gate posts and sang, '*St Peter don't allow no Cadillac drivers in here.*'

He tried to remember the correct version of the old spiritual as he drove along the dual carriageway, past acres of reclaimed land, where sports centres and shopping malls replaced the steelworks he had worked in for thirty-five years, before being made redundant. He was so busy trying to work out which department had stood on the new golf driving range, that he missed the turn-off at the roundabout and found himself travelling back down the dual carriageway towards town. After a volley of cursing and blaming the road signs for his mistake, he looked at his watch. The fingers standing at three o'clock reminded him of Pearl, on duty at the pedestrian crossing. He had an idea. Route 66 didn't close until six o'clock, so if he assured Pearl that he would return the car by then, it would give him three more hours. Three precious hours! It felt like a stay of execution. He slipped a tape into the player and celebrated with Danny and the Juniors 'At The Hop'.

Eddie was parked on the drive, putting his tattoos through their paces, when the artist called. Snakes and dragons writhed in mortal combat as he flexed his biceps. An eagle flapped its wings, and the little boy and girl who were standing by the car watching the show, ran away in terror when he made the lion roar. Eddie called them back, but they were already half way down the road and the sound of his voice made them run even faster. He shook his head and slapped the steering-wheel. He had messed up again. He just hoped that Pearl was still out when their mothers' called round to complain.

'Would you like your house painting, sir?'

Eddie had been so concerned about the fleeing children, that he hadn't noticed the young man standing by the gate. He couldn't be from the council. They just sent a letter telling you when they were starting.

'Sorry, mate, it's a council house. You're wasting your time round here. They're nearly all council houses on this estate.'

He didn't look like a council painter either, with his pony-tail and faded Megadeth T-shirt. Eddie recognized the name of the band, even though it was creased and partly concealed by the broad strap of the canvas bag across his chest. His son Danny had been a heavy metal fan and sometimes, when Eddie had burst into his bedroom to complain about the din, Danny would be standing over the record player, eyes closed, shaking his head in a frenzy. Sometimes he was so far gone that it required a thump to bring him back to his senses.

The young man adjusted the shoulder strap. The bag looked heavy. He looked like a paperboy setting off on his rounds.

'No. I don't mean painting your house. I mean would you like me to paint a picture of your house?'

The proposal was so absurd that Eddie glanced round for the hidden camera. Nobody was going to make a fool of him.

'You sound like a piss artist to me.'

He laughed and got out of the car. The young man wasn't amused. He shook his head vigorously.

'No. Straight up. Some people enjoy a picture of their house on the wall.'

'Yes, if it's Chatsworth House or somewhere like that. Not one of these fuckers though.'

'They do! You'd be surprised. It's a novelty. Like those aerial photographs that some people have taken.'

Eddie nodded. There was one on the wall in the Greyhound, but the photograph had been taken from so high up, that you needed a magnifying glass to identify the building.

The artist hitched up his bag and prepared to move on. Suddenly, Eddie felt sorry for him. The things people had to do to make a living these days; begging and busking and such like and doing crap jobs for fuck-all an hour. He had even seen one lad in town trying to walk across a rope tied between two trees. He fell off so often that passers-by thought it was a comedy act and the boy was embarrassed, even though they were throwing coins into his cap. Eddie wondered if the young man could paint him a picture of Elvis. Like the pavement artist outside the Black Swan. Even if it bore no resemblance to his idol, it would still be better than looking at a picture of his house.

'Nice car you've got there.'

'Thanks.'

'They certainly knew how to make them in those days.'

'They sure did.'

Eddie leaned against the door, including himself in the same vintage.

'It's a masterpiece. If you want something to paint, you ought to paint this.'

'Are you serious?'

It was more of a declaration than a proposition, but the more Eddie thought about it, the more he liked the idea. It would be a reminder, a souvenir. He might have owned it for only a day, but in a picture he would own it for ever.

'Can you paint cars?'

The artist laughed. 'I should hope so.'

'How about figures?'

'I can paint anything you like.'

'Right. Set your stall out. I'll be back in a minute.'

Eddie hurried into the house and the artist took out his folding easel and canvas stool from his bag and set them up on the lawn with the car in profile on the drive. He attached a sheet of drawing paper to the board with a bulldog clip, then placed a handful of pastel crayons in the tray.

Eddie emerged, wearing a clean T-shirt and his hair reinforced with Brylcreem in an attempt to support his sagging quiff.

'It's a good job it's not windy!' he shouted, keeping his head still as if he had got a stiff neck.

'Yes!' The artist shouted back to humour him, but with no idea what Eddie was talking about.

Eddie opened the car door then turned round.

'By the way, I forgot to ask. What do you charge?'

He charged according to the district and the house. Usually it was obvious how much the customer could afford, but this job was more complicated . . . council house, rough estate and the guy didn't look like the chairman of the board. Yet he owns this classic American limo which must have cost him. Perhaps he was one of those sentimental fools who had won the lottery and vowed that his new-found wealth would never change him. But weighing up the big slob before him, he doubted it. He looked like a guy who would move into a Barratt's mansion on a green-field site out of town and have a *string* of American cars on the driveway.

'Fifty pounds?'

'Piss off! I could get Picasso to paint me for that.'

'Forty.'

'Thirty.'

If the artist accepted this bid, he could pay him with a tenner and one of his half-price dud twenties, which meant that he would be getting the portrait for twenty pounds.

The artist hesitated. Eddie waited by the car.

'OK. Thirty. But I can't go lower than that.'

'Fair enough. We've all got a crust to earn.'

Eddie opened the car door and slid in.

'How do you want me, full face or in profile?'

'Well, as you're at the wheel, it would look more natural if you looked straight ahead.'

'Yes, I suppose so. What about a hat?'

'A hat? What kind of hat?'

'A cowboy hat.'

'Have you got one?'

'No, but I've got an old bush hat that belonged to my stepfather when he fought in the war. You could smarten it up a bit. You know, paint it white or something.'

'It's up to you. If you want to look like a cowboy, I'll paint you in a cowboy hat.' And if you want to look like a Red Indian, I'll paint you in a feathered head-dress, carrying a bow and arrow, he added under his breath.

His failure to gain recognition in the art world had made him cynical. After graduating from the Slade and dreaming of exhibitions in Milan and New York, he had been reduced to this, painting fat gits in flash cars on council estates.

Eddie turned his head as he considered himself in the windscreen mirror.

'Forget the hat. Paint me bare-headed.'

He had been called a cowboy often enough without giving credence to the insult.

'Perhaps you could paint me a bit more hair on though, you know, just thicken it up a bit and put a bit of gloss on, like Elvis's.'

It wasn't the most bizarre request he had ever received. One woman had wanted her house painted with her cat in the window. To give the picture a focal point, she said. Then she refused to pay him because she said it wasn't a good likeness. A good likeness! What did she expect? It was all black. A sooty smudge from fifty yards away. It would have been difficult to distinguish a lion at that distance.

'O K. How's this?'

Eddie sat with one hand on the steering-wheel and his arm resting on the car door, showing off his menagerie of tattoos.

'Yes, that's fine.'

And it was in this pose that Pearl saw him as she arrived home from work. Hot and tired and laden down with two heavy bags of shopping. Eddie saw her in the rear-view mirror as she turned into the drive. She was walking fast and he didn't like the look in her eyes and the way her jaw was thrust out. He felt sickeningly vulnerable when she disappeared from view, but he'd risk a battered skull rather than turn round and appear cowardly before the artist.

Pearl didn't edge carefully past the car this time, she strode straight down the border, leaving a trail of crushed flowers in her wake. Pity, Eddie thought, looking down at the flattened pansies, which he had transferred from his mother's garden. Still, it could have been worse. It could have been him! Pearl slammed the kitchen door so hard that the windows rattled and the neighbour's dog began to bark.

Sensing that he had been caught in the middle of a major domestic dispute, and that somehow he might be implicated, the artist worked fast. If the wife appeared again and he got out of the car to confront her, or if he suddenly jumped up and dashed into the house, there was no way that the sitting would be resumed and no way that the sitter would pay for a half-finished portrait. Eddie lit a cigarette, forgetful of his pose, but the artist, studying his tattooed fists and forearms, decided that perhaps it wasn't the right time to ask him to put it out and sit still.

'OK. It's finished.'

Eddie got out of the car, stepped over the squashed pansies, and stood behind the artist on the lawn. Just as Eddie had felt apprehensive when Pearl disappeared from the rear-view mirror and entered the blind spot behind him, the artist felt the same way as Eddie stared over his shoulder at the portrait. He didn't know what was going to happen next. A lengthy silence usually meant disappointment, followed by criticism and renegotiation of the fee.

'Do you like it?'

He remained facing the easel, trying to appear cool.

'Yeah. It's good. The motor's great.'

It was too. A great, red shark with gleaming fins stretched across the canvas. The artist had captured the flamboyant spirit of the car perfectly. Eddie was disappointed with his own portrait though. The clean-cut young dude he was expecting had been supplanted at the wheel by a boozy old rocker with heavy jowls. But after his initial disappointment, he reluctantly admitted the likeness. If the portrait was ever shown on *Crimewatch*, the switchboard would be jammed with callers.

'There's not much background is there?' Eddie asked, frowning at the grey wash behind the car. 'Why didn't you paint the privet in to add a bit of colour?'

The artist shrugged and looked up at Eddie.

'It's up to you. I can include it if you like, but in my opinion it will detract attention from the sitter and spoil the line of the car. A neutral background gives it cleaner definition and draws the viewer's eye.'

But Eddie wasn't convinced. It still looked half finished to him, and if he couldn't compete with a dusty, old privet hedge, he didn't have a lot going for him.

'What about some blue sky then to brighten it up a bit? You know, make it look like California. It looks as if it's going to piss it down with that grey background.'

'You never mentioned California.'

'I know. But when you're sat in this car, you imagine you're in California. You know, blue skies and all that.'

The artist picked up a blue pastel and shaded over the grey, accompanied by Eddie whistling 'Blue Skies' behind him.

'Yes. That's more like it.'

'Would you like a palm tree and a couple of beach babes to finish it off?'

Dealing with philistines was making him cynical. Eddie shook his head and laughed.

'You'd better not. I'm in enough trouble with the wife as it is.'

But as the grey sky turned blue, the artist had to admit that for once, the customer was right. The chrome work gleamed brighter, an additional smudge of white along the bonnet looked like reflected sunlight, and black shading underneath provided it with a shadow. Suddenly, the Cadillac was back in its natural setting. The artist began to sing 'I Get Around', even though he usually hated that surfin' shit, while Eddie stood silently beside him staring at the figure in the car. He gripped the hot steering-wheel as he gazed down the shimmering highway and he wished and he wished and he wished . . .

'Put me a Hawaiian shirt on.'

The artist laughed. He was enjoying his work for a change.

'What colour?'

'Anything. Just make it bright.'

The artist added a collar and loose sleeves to Eddie's T-shirt and coloured him like a parakeet.

'How's that?'

'Great. Give me some shades now. Wraparounds.'

'Are you sure you don't want the hat?'

'No. Who needs a hat with a head of hair like that?'

Finally, Eddie and the artist stood back and surveyed the finished work.

'You were right about the background. It brought it to life.'

Eddie took out a wad of bank notes from his back pocket.

'Yeah, well, you get enough grey skies in real life, don't you?'

After the artist had folded up his easel and left, Eddie remained on the lawn, admiring his portrait. How he envied himself sitting there. A real cool dude, dressed to kill and rarin' to go. The only place *he* was going, was back into the house to face Pearl.

He entered the living room, shaking his head and smiling at the picture in an effort to look relaxed. He considered offering it to Pearl as a gift, but decided that it would be a tactless gesture even by his standards.

'Have you seen this?'

He tried to sound cheerful, as if he had just read a heart-warming story in the newspaper. Pearl ignored him. She was sitting on the sofa, staring straight ahead, like a contestant in a 'Trying Not to Laugh' competition. Eddie wanted to share his pleasure with her, but he was afraid of what she might do to the picture if he took it within arm's length.

'What about the car?'

It was now Eddie's turn to ignore Pearl. He walked about the room, holding the picture up against the walls.

'It'll look lovely when I get it framed.'

'I thought you were taking it back.'

'What, already? I've only just had it painted.'

Pearl sat and waited for him to stop laughing. Eddie tried every feasible space on the walls before answering her question.

'I am.'

'When?'

'I was on my way when that painter fellow caught me. I was just pulling out of the drive.'

'Why didn't you take it back earlier? You've had all day.'

Pearl turned her head and looked at him. She waited. Eddie didn't have an answer. He looked down at the picture to avoid her gaze and he was sure that the fat bastard in the loud shirt was smirking behind his shades.

'You've no intention of taking it back, have you?'

He couldn't answer that one either.

'It's either the car or me. It's up to you.'

Eddie looked through the window at the temptress on the drive.

'It's the last straw, Eddie. You're totally irresponsible.'

The music started up again next door, and the bass beat thudded through the walls, causing ripples on the water in the goldfish bowl.

'Jesus fucking God!' Eddie roared at the wall.

'Never mind him. What about the car?'

'Fuck the car!'

'Don't you swear at me!'

'Well, shut up about it then! I'll please myself what I do!'

'You will not! If you think I'm working my fingers to the bone while you mess about in that . . . in that monstrosity.'

'Monstrosity.' Eddie was appalled. 'What are you talking about? It's beautiful! It's a work of art!'

Bhum. Bhum. Bhum. The beat came pounding through the wall.

'How much was it, anyway? You've never mentioned that.'

Eddie walked across to the window and fed the goldfish. The flecks of food quickly sank below the choppy surface.

'I'm waiting.'

Eddie stared through the window at the car. He was sweating. He lifted up the curtain and wiped his face.

'Well?'

'Stop nagging, will you?'

'I want to know!'

'All right then! Five! Six grand! So what?'

He released his rage by rushing across the room and hammering on the wall with his fist.

'Stop that bloody noise, will you?'

But the beat went on, with the dog joining in on vocals.

Pearl stared at Eddie, the din from next door forgotten.

'Six thousand pounds! That's your redundancy money. Don't tell me you've spent it all on that car?'

'So what? It's my money. I've worked for it.'

'It's our money, Eddie! It was our nest egg. Something to fall back on.'

Eddie glared around clenching his fists in frustration. Something was due through the window any second now. Pearl jumped up and faced him, aware that it might be her but too angry to care.

'That's it! That's the last straw! While I'm out working my fingers to the bone.' She held up her hand, stiff and trembling close to his face. 'You spend all day boozing, then blow every penny we've got on a stupid car!'

'I haven't been boozing.'

'Not much you haven't. I can smell it on your breath! I don't know why you don't pack your bags and go and live at the Greyhound.'

'What do you expect me to do, sit on my arse all day, listening to that racket? Shurrup!' he yelled at the wall.

'You could go out and look for a job for a start.'

'I do, for Christ's sake! I go down to the dole. I have interviews. I go on courses. But I'm going through the motions. They know it and I know it. I'm fifty-five years old and I'll never work again!' His anguished cry momentarily drowned the bass beat from next door. 'I was a skilled man. A craftsman.' He held out his hands, palms upward for inspection. 'Look at them. Just look at them. Useless. As soft as shit.' He turned them over, revealing bitten nails. 'Can you remember what they used to be like, when I was working? They were as tough as old boots. And all the little nicks and burns from flying sparks I used to get. I didn't care though, it was part and parcel of the job. That's what you get working with molten steel.' He touched the scars on his hands. 'We made the finest steel in the world. It made me feel proud when I saw all the countries that we used to export to: Japan, USA, Germany. We were giants then and I was part of it. Work's the main part of your life whatever people say, and when they take your work away, they take your life!'

Pearl was touched by his anguish, but her sympathy was tempered by the thought of the empty bank book and the white elephant parked on the drive.

'But what did you buy it for? We can't even afford an ordinary car, never mind that thing.'

'It's not *a thing*.'

'I mean, the size of it. It must cost a fortune to run.'

Eighteen miles to the gallon. But he daren't tell her that.

'I'll tell you why. Because it's fantastic. It's something to be proud of. It makes me feel like somebody when I'm driving it, instead of feeling like shit all the time. You've got to have something in your life, for Christ's sake!'

He turned away to hide his tears and stared out of the window at the car.

'We used to have this dream, me and Jet. Just taking off and driving across America to Graceland, in one of those big, flash cars we used to see in the pictures.'

It was Pearl's turn to dream now. She was in the car with Jet. He was wearing his blue suit, and she was wearing her polka-dot dress with the wasp-thin waist, and wide patent leather belt. It was hot and they were driving along a straight, lonely highway, listening to Chuck Berry on the radio. *Riding along in my automobile/Baby beside me at the wheel . . .*

'And look how I've finished up!'

Eddie's intervention brought her back home.

'A booby-prize husband! No job! And a nutter living next door.'

'Eddie! That's not fair! There was nothing between me and Jet!'

He ignored her and rushed from the room. Pearl closed her eyes and prayed silently. Anything could happen now.

Eddie returned, holding a sledgehammer. Pearl stepped behind the sofa, giving her a clear run to the door.

'Eddie?'

He leaned the handle carefully against the sideboard then started to take down the collection of family photographs from the dividing wall.

'Eddie.'

He took no notice and continued stacking the photographs on an armchair. Finally, he unhooked the mirror from above the fireplace and cleared the ornaments from the mantelpiece. The sequence of clean squares where the photographs had hung looked like stepping stones across a river.

'Eddie! What are you doing?'

Glancing from the sledgehammer to the bare wall, his intention seemed obvious, but she still couldn't believe it. She knew what he was capable of when he lost his temper, but this was extreme behaviour even by his standards.

'Stand back.'

As Pearl was already standing behind the sofa, his instructions were superfluous. But when she saw him spit on his palms and pick up the sledgehammer, she ran for the door.

'Eddie, don't!'

She considered phoning the police, but if they arrived

before he had worked out his rage, he might have blue murder on his hands. It was safer to take it out on their noisy neighbour than take it out on them.

The first blow crushed a gondolier on the wallpaper. The second smashed his boat and plaster spilled to the floor. Pearl wondered whether to run upstairs for some dust sheets, but she was afraid that this might enrage him further and he would smash up the furniture too.

Eddie swung the sledgehammer strongly and rhythmically and after a few blows he was through to the brickwork. He had worked in the demolition business after being made redundant, but when they were contracted to destroy the buildings in which he had worked all his life, he couldn't face it and he handed in his notice.

The music continued next door even while Eddie was attacking the wall. His neighbour was cursing and shouting and banging back and the dog was barking hysterically. But Eddie ignored them. He picked up the beat and hammered in time. The walls shook at every blow. The windows rattled. The light shade tinkled and the goldfish battled through choppy waters.

'For God's sake, Eddie! That's enough!'

Eddie ignored her. The lamp on the television wobbled. The heavy glass ashtray slid across the polished surface of the sideboard, and the pyramid of apples fell out of the fruit dish and rolled on to the floor. Red dust filled the air and a pile of plaster built up against the wall. Eddie was sweating and panting and his flabby muscles ached, but fury kept him going and he grunted with satisfaction when he felt a brick dislodge and a hole appeared in the wall. A compressed howl of music exploded through the gap, accompanied by frenzied barking and screamed insults. Eddie stepped back and narrowed his eyes against the blast as if he was staring into a furnace. The dog's snarling jaws appeared at the hole. It looked as if it was about to chew the bricks and scramble through. Eddie spat on his palms and took a fresh grip on the sledgehammer.

'Call it off or I'll kill it!'

Eddie couldn't tell what the man said over the barking and loud music, but it didn't sound like 'sit'. Eddie swung the hammer at the course of bricks below the dog's head and there was a chilling howl as the wall caved in, followed by fading yelps as the dog fled from the house. Moments later, the dog's owner appeared at the hole, threatening Eddie with the police and RSPCA. Eddie swung his sledgehammer again, forcing him back under a shower of bricks and plaster, then he pursued him through the hole, intent on revenge.

A pair of giant speakers flanked three young children watching television on the sofa. They barely looked up when Eddie appeared, as if visitors entering the house through the wall was an everyday occurrence. Their father was panicking. Banging on the walls and threats over the privet he could handle, but a lunatic on the loose with a sledgehammer was a different matter. He was standing at the front door calling the dog when he heard the first thud followed by a reduction in the volume of the music. Seconds later, the music stopped altogether and he ran back inside when he heard the television explode, passing his wailing children on their way out.

Both speakers and the television had been smashed in, and the man was looking to see if his video library of kung-fu classics was still intact, when Eddie grabbed him by the throat.

'You bastard!'

The man kept his hands by his side.

'You lay a finger on me and I'll call the police.'

'Call the police!' Eddie laughed, head-butting him in the face. 'If the police searched this house, you'd get life.'

Pearl, watching fearfully through the hole in the wall, screamed when she saw the blood spread across the man's face.

'Eddie! Stop it! That's enough!'

The man felt his nose, then stared at his blood-stained fingers.

'You've broken it! You've broken my fucking nose!'

'Yes, and I'll break your fucking neck next time.'

Pearl scrambled through the hole and grabbed Eddie's arm.

'That's enough, Eddie. You'll get in trouble.'

'He's in trouble already,' the neighbour said in a muffled voice, as he tried to staunch the blood with his T-shirt.

Pearl turned on him, appalled at his stupidity.

'If I was you I'd keep quiet, unless you want to end up with three orphans.'

Eddie pushed her away.

'You keep out of it. It's none of your business.'

'Of course it's my business! I don't want to be visiting Armley for the next twenty years if you do him in.'

'That's typical of you.'

'What is?'

'Thinking about yourself as usual.'

'Me! Working every hour that God sends. It's me that's kept us going for the past five years.'

'That's it, rub it in.'

'Don't you dare call me selfish when you've just spent every penny we've got on a heap of old junk!'

'I wondered when that'd come up.'

'It'll keep coming up until you've taken it back!'

'Put me down, will you? I think I'm going to pass out.'

Eddie had forgotten all about his battered neighbour, suspended by the throat with his Nike trainers barely touching the floor.

'And you!' He refocused his aggression and tightened his grip. 'If I hear one more sound through that wall . . .' Eddie pushed him across the room and slammed him against the wall so hard, that another brick fell out. 'I'll break every bone in your fucking body!'

Eddie released him. The man slid down the wall and lay still in the rubble. Eddie gave him a parting kick then ducked back through the hole into his own living room. Pearl started screaming behind him.

'You've killed him! Call an ambulance. Eddie! He's dead!'

Eddie kept going. Out through the kitchen into the car. He didn't believe her. He had dished out much worse beatings than that and seen his opponent back at the bar twenty minutes later. As he backed out of the drive, Eddie saw his neighbour's children comforting their trembling dog on the front lawn.

Eddie pushed a button on the dashboard and the hood closed over him, then he cruised around the estate trying to work out his next move. What if he *had* killed Jacko? Perhaps he ought to make a run for it. What, in a red Cadillac? He'd be less noticeable driving a fire engine. The police would pick him up before he'd left town. Perhaps he ought to ditch it and borrow a less conspicuous model to make his getaway, an Escort or a Cavalier. But as he ran his hands around the steering-wheel and looked down the long, gleaming bonnet, he knew he couldn't do it. If he was going to prison, he wanted to be arrested in style. The police would respect a guy who drove a car like this. He could see them getting out of their patrol cars and taking in the details as they walked towards him; the massive chrome fender, the white-wall tyres and matching white hood. They would lift up the bonnet and enthuse over the engine before taking him in.

He heard a police car in the distance. Or was it an ambulance on its way to pick up his dead neighbour? His time was up. Would Pearl visit him in jail? Perhaps he had gone too far this time and she would sue him for divorce. How long would he get? Ten? No. Fifteen years at least, even though he had been severely provoked. He would take up a hobby to pass the time, like Burt Lancaster in *The Bird Man of Alcatraz*. Perhaps he could study motor mechanics and become an expert on classic American cars. He was wondering if anybody would visit him if he was imprisoned hundreds of miles away on the Isle of Wight, when he saw Betty waving to him from the pavement outside her house. He pulled up opposite the gate, and when she leaned over in a low-cut sweater, he forgot all about going to prison.

'It's fantastic, Eddie!'

'Yeah. Thanks.'

'A few people have told me they'd seen you driving around in a flashy car. I didn't expect it to be anything like this though.'

Betty stepped back to take in the full length of the car.

'It's so big!'

That's nothing. You should see the size of this, Eddie thought, dropping his hands over his crotch.

'All you need now is a cowboy hat.'

Betty stroked the hood and peered inside.

'I love the white upholstery. It's so classy. You'll have to give me a ride sometime.'

Eddie was tempted to open the door there and then despite what the neighbours would say. Anyway, what did it matter after what had just happened? Pearl wouldn't care. It was all over now. She would find somebody else. She was still attractive. He'd noticed the way that men looked at her. Young guys too . . . Bastards!

'What have you done to your hands? It looks as if you've committed a murder.'

Eddie unclenched his fists from the steering-wheel and stared at them. It was the first time he had noticed the blood.

'You've got blood on your T-shirt as well.'

'Yeah . . . Next door's dog got knocked down and I've just taken it to the vet's. The bloke who owns it couldn't go. He had an accident. He's in bed.'

'Why don't you come in and wash your hands? You'll feel better.'

Eddie was tempted for the second time. Oh, how he was tempted. He imagined the scenario. It was like one of those blue videos that he sometimes watched at Ronnie's house after the pub . . . When they were inside Betty would say, 'Why don't you take a bath, Eddie? You look tired. It'll help you relax.' Then, as he was lying there, covered in Radox bubbles, there would be a soft knock on the door and Betty would enter, wearing . . . But he was too upset to continue, and when he thought of Pearl lying in the bath with her new boyfriend, his expression was so fearsome that Betty looked down the road to see what he was staring at.

'What's the matter?'

After he had brained Pearl's boyfriend with the towel rail, Eddie relaxed his grip on the steering-wheel and shook his head.

'Oh, nothing. Anyway, thanks Betty. I'd better be going.'

'OK, Eddie.' Betty stepped back from the car. 'Anytime. You know where I am.'

'I see you've got a new fence.'

He nodded towards the raw palings which had been erected across the gap where the privet hedge had stood.

'Yes. They did it today. I was just inspecting it when you came past. It's a pity they're not iron, then the next buggers that go through it'd finish up kebabed.'

As Eddie drove away, he remembered the approaching police siren just before he had stopped at Betty's. It couldn't have been heading for Jacko's house after all, or he would have been under arrest by now. So he wasn't dead after all. The bastard! Scaring the life out of him like that. He cruised around for a while wondering what to do next. Then he stopped alongside the recreation ground, lowered the hood and lit a cigarette. It was too late to return the car now, but he daren't take it home. Not again. It would seem like sheer provocation. He wasn't even sure if *he* would be welcome, never mind the car. He could take it to his son Danny's, or to any of his mates' houses; they would park it up for the night. But he didn't like the idea of it being exposed on a drive at the other side of the estate, and he couldn't think of anybody with a garage big enough to lock it up in. But it was more than that. He was making excuses. The truth was that he didn't want to be parted from the car. It was too painful, like the reluctant, but inevitable end of a passionate affair.

Eddie gazed across the recreation ground and watched the children swarming over the swings and climbing frame. He rested his head against the back of the seat and closed his eyes, and remembered when he used to bring Danny and Jane to play on the swings and kick a ball around with them on the grass. Those were the good years, when he was earning high wages in the rolling mill and working hard for the family.

He smelled burning plastic, opened his eyes and sat up. Somebody had set one of the swings on fire and the children were running away across the football pitch. At first, they were all spread out like the start of a cross-country race, but when they noticed the car, they converged into a phalanx then flowed around it like a river round a stone. Eddie watched them closely as they milled about him, the burned swing already forgotten.

'No touching. I've just polished it.'

Eddie looked at their faces. He didn't know any of them. When Danny and Jane were their age, and their friends were in and out of the house all the time, he seemed to know every child on the estate. These days, he hardly knew any of them on his street.

'Where've you got it from, mister?'

The boy, wearing a pair of football shorts and trainers, was dancing around and laughing at his rubbery reflection in the polished door. Eddie was transported back to the Hall of Mirrors in the pleasure beach at Blackpool and planning to push Jack off the Big Dipper.

'America.'

'Did you go there to buy it?'

Eddie hesitated.

'Yeah. It belonged to a friend. He was stationed over here during the war.'

By this time, all the children had gathered at Eddie's side of the car.

A girl in a baseball cap said, 'My grandad was in the war.'

A boy with a ferret round his neck, said:

'Mine was. He was killed by the Japs.'

When he was their age, Eddie used to wish that his stepfather had been killed by the Japs too, then he wouldn't have come home and spoiled everything . . . It was time to change the subject before he grew morose.

'Who's heard of Elvis Presley?'

'Me!' they chorused, and one boy instinctively raised his hand as if he was at school.

'He was a singer.'

Others added quick-fire contributions.

'Rock 'n' roll!'

'*Jailhouse Rock*! It was on the telly.'

'Elvis the pelvis!'

'What's the pelvis?' a boy in a Manchester United strip asked.

The children glanced around at each other but nobody knew and the pause allowed Eddie to continue.

'Well, according to my friend, this car,' patting the door, 'belonged to Elvis himself.'

There were intakes of breath, low whistles and reverential murmurs at this disclosure, and a little girl wearing Dracula teeth said, 'Just think, you're sitting where Elvis sat.'

Eddie hadn't thought of that but he was happy to sustain the myth. 'That's right.' He hesitated, searching for a royal metaphor. 'I'm sitting on the King's throne.'

The children peered over the car door at the white upholstery then gazed at Eddie in awe. He smiled at a boy wearing a clapping hands cap, then released the hand brake and put the car into drive. It was time to go before one of them broke the spell with an awkward question.

Eddie *was* Elvis as he drove across the estate towards Memphis, Tennessee, and when he entered the Greyhound he was walking into Sam Phillip's Sun Records studio to cut his next disc. He tried to maintain his rôle by selecting all the Elvis records on the juke box, but when he heard the opening bars of 'Always On My Mind', he was singing to Pearl and not Priscilla.

He stood at the end of the bar on his own, smoking and drinking heavily all evening. He refused offers to play cards, darts or pool, and when the landlord called 'Time!' and then, twenty minutes later, 'Have you no homes to go to?', Eddie stared morosely into the mirror behind the optics, wondering whether he had or not.

He was last out, and as he stumbled down the steps and lurched sideways across the car park, he realized that he couldn't possibly go home now, not in this state. Pearl had probably locked him out anyway, and she wouldn't be too happy if he smashed the door in, especially after the damage he had inflicted on the living-room wall. He stroked the soft hood of his car like a cow puncher greeting his trusty old steed, then unlocked the door and flopped inside. Now what? He was too drunk to drive so he would have to stay here and sleep it off. Pearl wouldn't care where he slept. She wouldn't care if he never came home again. She'd be glad. She wished he was dead. The police phoning up. It's bad news, I'm afraid. He's been involved in a car crash. Eddie lay down on the seat with his hands across his chest and sang the first verse of 'Crying In The Chapel', before falling asleep and dreaming about Jet and Pearl. They were jiving together, then his mother appeared, waving to him across the dance floor. He woke up trembling and sweating and raised his arm to try to catch the light from the street lamps on his watch. But he was too drunk and dizzy to focus and he closed his eyes and gripped the steering-wheel to steady himself on the rough sea. He dreamt of Jack. He was wearing his army uniform and carrying a kitbag on his shoulder. Eddie began to shake his head. 'No, Dad! No!' A prowler in a hooded sweatshirt appeared outside and padded round the car. He glanced inside and saw a big man – he looked like a bouncer in civvies – lying on the front seat, having a fit. 'Please, Dad . . .' Jack was unbuckling his belt and pulling it through the loops. Raising his arm. 'No! No!' Eddie jerked up and stared wildly through the window. The hooded figure leapt back in terror and fled across the car park, clearing the wall like a hurdler before disappearing into the estate.

For a moment Eddie didn't know where he was. Then he remembered and opened his eyes. But the clear morning light was too bright and he was forced to close them again. He lay on the seat and gave himself a check-up: pounding skull, knackered, thirsty, sick stomach and a tongue like a fur rug. Nothing abnormal. Just the usual symptoms after a heavy night out. He pulled himself up with the steering-wheel, put on his sunglasses, then lowered the hood and inhaled deep breaths of cool morning air. In the distance, the sun was rising above the new business park and it was still quiet enough to hear the cascading notes of a robin from the roof of the leisure centre across the road.

Eddie squinted at his watch: six twenty-five. It was safe to go home now as Pearl would have left for work. As he drove across the estate, he recalled his dreams with their familiar characters and confused narratives of suffering and loss. But what about the new character: the grim reaper peering down at him from under his hood? Perhaps it was a warning to mend his ways, to stop smoking and drinking so heavily, or the figure in the hood would be calling again. Eddie was still worrying about it when he arrived home, but he forgot all about his unwelcome visitor as he concentrated on the more important business of easing the car between the gate posts without scratching the paintwork.

It seemed ominous that Pearl hadn't left him a note on the kitchen table. Even a rebuke would have been better than nothing. He walked into the living room but the table in there was bare too. Pearl had cleared away the rubble and wedged a sheet of hardboard over the hole in the wall with the sideboard. As Eddie surveyed the makeshift repair, the term 'broken home' came to mind.

He returned to the kitchen and opened the fridge door. He was ravenous. He hadn't had anything to eat since yesterday lunchtime, except for a bag of crisps and a packet of pork scratchings in the pub. So he tried to comfort himself with a fry-up, supplemented with a pot of tea and half a loaf of sliced bread, stacked up at the side of his plate like bathroom tiles. But he didn't enjoy it. He was hung-over, tired and unhappy.

He lit a cigarette, poured another mug of tea then sat staring out of the window into the back garden. The dahlias and roses were in full bloom and the gladioli were coming into flower, unlike Eddie, who was fading fast.

He cleared the table then washed up. After the events of the previous day, he didn't relish the prospect of Pearl arriving home and finding his greasy pots in the sink. As he spread out the tea towel to hang it up to dry, he noticed that it was decorated with a map of the British Isles featuring obvious tourist destinations. London was symbolized by a pike-bearing beefeater, Edinburgh by a kilted piper and Stratford-on-Avon by the familiar bust of Shakespeare. Main rivers and mountain ranges were included and as Eddie zipped haphazardly around the country, he began to sing, '*Riding along in my automobile/Baby beside me at the wheel/ Listening along on my radio/No particular place to go.*' And then! He stopped singing. He knew! He knew what he was going to do! Where he was going! Suddenly, he *had* a particular place to go. He could feel his heart pumping with excitement and he lit another cigarette to calm himself down. It was a stupid! crazy! mad idea! He had to agree. But what an adventure it would be to fulfil that distant dream.

But he had to move fast. He had to be gone before Pearl returned and doused his enthusiasm. As soon as she walked in, the interrogation would begin. When was he taking the car back? What was he going to do about the damaged wall? Where had he been all night? Before he knew what had happened, he would be back on the sofa, watching *The Big Breakfast* on television.

He scribbled a note to Pearl on a gas bill envelope, telling her that he had gone away for a couple of days and not to worry, he would be back soon. As he was locking the kitchen door behind him, he suddenly remembered something. 'Please, please,' he muttered fearfully as he rushed back inside and through to the living room. He paused for an instant, then, fearing the worst, yanked open the sideboard drawer. But there it was, still in one piece between the pages of his mother's photograph album: his portrait at the wheel of his car. He was afraid that Pearl might have torn it up in revenge. Perhaps she hadn't found it. But she must have, because she had emptied the cupboards before wrestling the sideboard across the room to cover the hole in the wall. Suddenly Eddie was overcome with gratitude and love and he was ashamed of himself for even thinking that Pearl could be capable of such a vindictive act. He imagined himself in her position; if he had found the picture in the drawer, he would have ripped it into so many pieces that she would have had to suck them up with the vacuum cleaner. He picked up the album containing the portrait, then, as he turned to leave the room, the darting movements of the goldfish caught his eye. He sprinkled fish food into the bowl then tapped the glass with his fingernail as a parting gesture.

'So long, Jaws. It's now or never, as the King used to sing.'

Eddie's heart thumped with excitement as he drove across the estate, listening to the powerful rumble of the pent-up engine. He passed a blown safe, a burned-out car, and a saddled horse grazing on a grass verge. When he passed Betty's house, he noticed that her new fence had disappeared. He turned on to the main road and joined the flow of the early morning traffic into town. It was time to open up. He pressed the button on the dashboard and listened to the hum of the hood retracting. He loved it: the brilliant exposure. He was a star, caught by the spotlight as the curtains slid back. It was time for some music. '*Lucille!*' Little Richard screamed as Eddie pulled up at a set of traffic lights, prompting the driver in the next lane to close his windows. Eddie grinned across at him but he looked away. Stuck-up bastard in his pin stripes and Jag. But he didn't care. He didn't care about any of them now, whatever they were wearing or driving. But he used to, when he went into town to visit the Job Centre or to sign on. He would stare enviously at the BMWs and Mercs with striped umbrellas and pig-skin briefcases in the back. But he didn't feel like that now. People were staring at *him*. For the first time in years, he felt like somebody again.

Eddie parked the car outside a row of shops, bought a newspaper and a pack of cigarettes from the newsagent's, then went into the café next door and sat at the window with a cup of tea. As he scanned the paper, he listened to two boys wearing baseball caps and baggy trousers sitting at the next table. 49ers instructed Yankees how to make gas meters run backwards in order to obtain free gas. Then with the aid of the salt pot, Yankees demonstrated the correct way to climb through a cat flap.

Eddie kept glancing out of the window and smiling at the car. He noticed that most of the people who walked past it smiled too. It was big and bold and brazen. It was Top of the Pops, King of the Castle, the bee's knees, number 1. It was the car which led the procession through town. Eddie noticed that it was standing in front of a bank, which made it look even more imposing. He would have liked a few snapshots of it to impress his mates. They would assume that he was conducting business inside, rather than sitting in a cheap café opposite. He wondered if the two lads at the next table might have a camera handy, and even if they hadn't, he knew that it wouldn't take them long to produce one. But he resisted the temptation. He wanted to be on his way. If he sat around for too long, he might change his mind and turn back. He looked at his watch, finished his tea and left the café.

The Tiger Tattoo parlour was situated between a charity shop and a bookmaker's, a few minutes' walk along the road. It had been converted from a fish and chip shop and the frosted glass door panel was engraved with a galleon and a flying fish. During one session under the needle, Max, the tattoo artist and owner of the establishment, had told Eddie that one new customer had been so confused by the choice of designs around the walls that, in desperation, he had finally settled for a galleon on one bicep and a flying fish on the other.

The door was locked. Eddie knocked and rattled the letter box until he saw a dark form behind the glass and heard the rasp of bolts being withdrawn.

'Hang on, for Christ's sake! What you trying to do, knock the bloody door down?'

Max was expecting trouble when he opened the door. He was ready for a confrontation with a drunk, or a junkie bent on some desperate commission, or an irate mother demanding the immediate removal of a naked woman from the arm of her teenage son. When he saw Eddie standing on the door step, he was relieved but still annoyed. In his black T-shirt, with his greying hair fastened back in a pony-tail, he looked like a roadie in a heavy metal band.

'Bloody hell, Eddie. I don't open till ten, you know. What's the rush?'

Max, who lived over the shop, yawned and blinked in the bright morning sunlight. Eddie stepped inside and closed the door.

'I'm in a hurry.'

'What's up, robbed a bank?'

'I'd hardly be stopping for a tattoo if I'd robbed a bank, would I?'

'I don't know. I get some right weirdos in here. I once had a kid wanted a Lone Ranger mask tattooed on his face.'

'Did you do it?'

'Did I fuck. I told him to fuck off: Tonto!'

The shop was still divided by the counter, but the pans had been removed and replaced by a sink and worktop for Max's equipment. Chairs had been placed against the walls where the customers used to queue, but now, instead of ordering cod and chips, they studied the design sheets covering the walls and ordered pierced hearts, Indian chiefs, and bulldogs dressed in Union Jacks.

Max lifted the counter flap and Eddie followed him through into his studio.

'What do you want this time then?'

'A number.'

'A number? What sort of number?'

Eddie picked up a Biro from the counter and printed it on the cover of an *Autosport* magazine: 53310761. Max studied it for a few moments then shook his head.

'What is it, your pools numbers or something?'

'I can't tell you. It's a secret.'

'Where do you want it, then? On your arse where nobody can see it?'

Eddie sat on a chair and pulled up the sleeve of his T-shirt over his shoulder.

'There. Put it there. There's just enough room.'

He tapped his arm above the spread eagle on his bicep. Max shaved the area with a disposable razor, sprayed it with an antiseptic solution, then lightly printed the number on Eddie's arm with the Biro.

'How's that look?'

Eddie raised his arm and looked at the number upside down, then looked into the wall mirror and saw it in reverse.

'Yeah, that's great.'

Max plugged the tattoo gun into a wall socket, dipped the needle into a pot of blue ink and began to prick out the number, dabbing continuously with a sheet of kitchen roll to absorb the wet ink and blood. As he worked, Eddie studied the tattoos on Max's hands and forearms. The designs were so intricately entwined that he looked as if he was wearing long lace gloves.

'Have you done any numbers before?'

'Now and again. Girlfriends' birthdays and that. A bloke came in last week wanting Combat 18 on his skull. I told him to fuck off. I don't do swastikas either. I won't have anything to do with that stuff.'

Max unplugged the machine and stood up.

'That's it. All done and dusted.'

Eddie looked in the mirror and flexed his bicep for a wide screen effect.

'Five double three one o seven six one,' he repeated like a mantra.

Max folded a clean sheet of kitchen roll and sellotaped it over the tattoo, as if he was going to test Eddie's memory.

'Keep that on for a couple of hours and don't forget to keep it clean until it's healed up.'

'Yeah, I know. How much do I owe you?'

'A fiver.'

Eddie nodded towards a sheet of designs on the wall behind the piercing bench.

'I'm going to have one of them next time.'

'What?'

'An arrow through the heart.'

'They're always popular.'

'I can imagine.'

'A feller came in last week asking if I could do one with a dagger through it.'

Eddie picked up his sunglasses and cigarettes from the counter.

'I know just how he feels.'

As Eddie walked back to the car, he thought about Pearl. She would have returned from her morning shift on the school crossing by now. He could see her at home, sitting at the kitchen table with a mug of tea, reading his note. What was she thinking? How would she respond? He tried anger first. She ripped up the note then threw the teapot against the wall. He didn't like this scene at all. It was X-rated material. He glanced over his shoulder to make sure she wasn't on his tail. Next, grief. She was devastated, sobbing into her hands. No, it was too extreme. She had never broken down like that. Not even when her mother died. But what about the night that Jet was killed? She broke down then.

But that was understandable after what had happened, he tried to convince himself. Finally, he tried regret. Yes, that struck the right melancholy note. He could see her staring sadly across the kitchen with the note in her hand. Yes, that's how she would be. Not furious, or grief stricken, but sad, reflecting on their life together, their ups and downs, the growing tensions which had driven them apart.

Eddie was sad too, in spite of the novelty of his new tattoo. Except for a few months working away after he had been made redundant, this was the first time they had been separated since their marriage. How he had missed her, and he had never messed around chasing women like some of the other guys. Pearl was enough for him. He loved her the first time they met and he had loved her ever since.

He was tempted to phone her. Or even return home. What if she was already celebrating his departure with a can of Special Brew? What if she was seeing a fancy man on the quiet and moved in with him while he was away? But in spite of his rising panic he couldn't return yet. Not after his farewell note and dramatic exit. He would look pathetic walking back into the house carrying the photograph album and portrait, and a sheet of flowered kitchen roll taped to his arm.

Anyway, he was only going for a couple of days. It was a defiant gesture to restore hurt pride. Pearl was right about the car, he realized that, but he wanted to enjoy it for a little while before he took it back. He couldn't keep dawdling around the estate in it. It was a waste, like keeping a racehorse in the back yard.

Thinking about the car and his imminent journey made him excited. It was like going to the cinema when he was a child, that same thrilling promise which, at times, became so powerful that he would run until he saw the domed roof of the Alhambra, and only then would he slow down, relieved that it had not somehow vanished since his last visit.

Eddie took out his car keys and looked along the line of parked vehicles. He couldn't see his car. It must be further along the road, behind the removal van which was blocking his view. He walked faster, resisting the temptation to run, but when he reached the van and he looked up the road he realized that his car, unlike the Alhambra, *had* vanished! Keep calm! Don't panic! he ordered, suddenly drenched in sweat. I don't believe it. I don't fucking believe it, he kept repeating to himself, shaking his head. As he stood there, sick and bewildered, wondering what to do next, he was distracted by a frenzy of hammering and drilling from a derelict chapel across the road. Hang on! Eddie took in the scaffolding, the bulldozer and the poster on the notice board announcing the opening of a new theme pub called the Holy Roller. He hadn't passed this on the way down. He was certain. He would have noticed it straight away with all the noise and activity taking place. He looked along the road and grinned with relief. If somebody had stolen his car, they must have stolen the bank too! Some robbery, Eddie thought, retracing his steps. He had been so busy thinking about Pearl when he left the tattoo studio that he had turned in the wrong direction.

He hurried back, relieved yet still anxious, as if waking from a nightmare. As he passed the tattoo studio, a scowling boy emerged, slamming the door behind him, before giving the shop the V-sign and running away. Eddie quickened his pace, scanning the line of parked vehicles ahead . . . *Yes!*

There she was, waiting outside the bank. His heart bumped with relief. It was like his first date with Pearl: the bowel-churning anxiety, foiled by the burst of elation when he saw her waiting for him outside the Alhambra. But as he drew closer, he noticed two youths loitering by the car. One of them was stroking the bonnet while the other peered inside.

'Oi!' Eddie started to run. He accelerated past the pawn-broker's and the Pride of Bombay, an awesome sight, a baby bulldozer, a runaway truck, steaming along the pavement, barging pedestrians aside. The two youths turned and watched him approach. They had heard the shout but didn't know at whom it was directed, but when he roared 'Bastards!' and shook his fist as he thundered towards them, they realized that it was directed at them. They didn't wait to explain that they were only admiring the car; in his state he wouldn't have believed them. So they dodged across the busy road, opting for the dangers of the speeding cars in preference to the threat of the on-rushing nutter.

Eddie flopped against the side of the car, arms outstretched, head resting on the roof like a suspect about to be frisked. He couldn't breathe. His heart was bursting. He needed a fag. He needed a drink. He needed to lie down. He had saved his car in vain. He was about to die on it. Passers-by thought he was having a fit of some description, but nobody stopped to help him. He was a big, tough-looking sod and they weren't sure how he would react.

Gradually, as his heart slowed down and he regained his breath, he realized that he was going to live. He smiled, eyes closed, enjoying the warmth of the hood on his cheek. She was safe. His precious. His beauty. He stood up straight and ripped the crude dressing from his tattoo.

'OK, baby. Let's go!' he yelled, climbing into the car. When he pressed the button and the hood folded back, it was like leaving the cinema on a sunny afternoon. He eased his way into the traffic then selected a Fats Domino tape and passed through 'Kansas City' and 'My Blue Heaven' before pulling into a filling station on the edge of town.

He put twenty pounds' worth of petrol in the tank then swaggered into the shop with his thumbs down his belt.

'Howdy, ma'am.'

The young woman behind the counter nodded towards the Cadillac, which was filling all the spaces by the pumps.

'I like your car.'

'Thank you kindly.'

Eddie picked up a bag of Opal Fruits and a Mars bar from the shelves and placed them on the counter.

'Are you American?'

'I sure am.'

The attendant looked doubtfully at his Boddingtons T-shirt and Union Jack tattoo.

'Where are you from?'

'Way down south in the land of cotton.' He almost broke into a rendition of 'Dixie', but managed to pull back in time. 'Memphis, Tennessee, to be exact.'

'Fancy that. That's where Elvis lived, isn't it?'

'You're darn right he did!' Eddie yelled, slapping his thigh and almost giving a yahoo! 'I live just down the road from Graceland itself.'

'Do you? I've got a friend who's been to Graceland. She says she was surprised how small it was.'

'Yeah, well . . . Maybe so, maybe so.'

Eddie was taken aback. He had imagined Graceland to

be as grand as the White House. It was time to change the subject before she went into detail and exposed his pretence.

'I'm over here on vacation, visiting my son.'

'That's nice. We don't get many Americans round here.'

'There were a lot of Americans round during the war. They were based out at Wharncliffe.'

'Fancy! I never knew that.'

'A bit before your time, I would guess, ma'am.'

He smiled hoping she might return the compliment. But she ignored him and tapped up his bill. Eddie counted off the notes from the wad in his back pocket.

'The old country's a midy expensive place to visit these days. The exchange rate sucks.'

The attendant slid Eddie's change across the counter.

'I wouldn't know. The only exchange I ever see is *Exchange and Mart*.'

Eddie picked up his sweets.

'Bye now. In the immortal words of Jerry Lee Lewis, I'd bedder be "Movin' On Down The Line".'

As Eddie walked away, the attendant noticed the label on the back pocket of his jeans and started to laugh. He hadn't bought those in Memphis, Tennessee. He'd bought them from Asda!

'Have a nice day!' she called as he reached the door.

'*Going to take a sentimental journey*,' Eddie sang as he headed out of town towards the site of the old American air force base. He drove through the devouring suburbs, where each phase of post-war architectural fashion was as clearly defined as rings on a tree trunk. Then, after a notice board announcing an exclusive development of executive dwellings, he was out in the countryside, driving between meadows and fields of ripe corn.

He tried to imagine the road during the war, when it was busy with supply trucks and staff cars, and Jeeps packed with rowdy airmen in leather jackets, waving and hollering at their low-flying aircraft as they roared overhead. As he approached the site of the airfield, he decided that 'My Ding-A-Ling' was inappropriate, disrespectful even, to commemorate his visit, so he switched off the tape and whistled 'American Patrol', giving it the full Glenn Miller treatment inside his head.

He stopped by a derelict barn, then got out of the car and stood gazing across the fields. He used to cycle out here when he was a boy and look over the hedge, just like he was looking over it now. Remains of the airbase were still visible then: the derelict gatehouse, the concrete floor of the hangar and the crumbling runway, sprouting thistles and grass. But when Eddie looked down the runway, he didn't notice the weeds. He saw Flying Fortresses lumbering into the air on bombing missions over Germany. Then he would stand there, staring into the sky until his neck ached as he waited for them to return. And then he would spot one, and sometimes he would get so excited by this first sighting that he would shout, 'There!' and point it out to the ground crew waiting anxiously by the ambulance. Some returned safely, with the pilot removing his helmet and waving as he emerged from the cockpit. Some 'limped back on a wing and a prayer' as they said in the war films. He would hear the ailing engines first, phut-phutting as they threatened to die. Then it would come into view, with smoke streaming from the tail. 'Please, God. Please, God,' Eddie would whisper as it came in to land with its undercarriage shot away and a wing on fire. He screwed up his face as it screeched, sparks flying, along the runway with the fire engine racing towards it. And sometimes they didn't return at all and he stood there clutching his mother's silver dollar and staring at the sky, whispering, 'Come back. Please come back.'

And now, nearly fifty years later, Eddie wiped away the tears on his tattooed hands and squeezed the silver dollar so hard that it left an imprint on his palm. He stood to attention and saluted, watching a skylark rise from the meadow. He held his stance until it disappeared from view, then he returned to the car, closed the hood and put on his sunglasses. He needed privacy, time to reflect and recover. After three cigarettes he felt calm enough to begin his journey north.

Eddie didn't need a map, he knew the route off by heart. He could see the long red line bisecting the shades of green and brown, and he could still recite the places along the way like a poem. There was a faster, more direct route by motorway now, but Eddie ignored the signs and headed for the old A1, to begin the journey he had planned with Jet when the songs on his tapes were still in the hit parade.

They used to study the map leaning over the table in Eddie's living room. He had borrowed the atlas from school when he became interested in America, then failed to return it when he left. He would lie on the rug in front of the fire, roaming the country from the plains of Montana to the cotton fields of Mississippi. He knew each state by its jigsaw-puzzle shape and he learned off by heart the names of the rivers and mountains . . . Then his mother would look up anxiously from her sewing when she heard Jack come in, and Eddie would casually turn the pages and pretend to be looking at

Africa or Asia. He studied the map of America so often that the atlas opened automatically at that page and later, when planning their Scottish adventure, he had to hold down the pages to prevent them turning back.

Eddie released the hood, his excitement growing as he saw signs indicating the A1. He stopped at a set of traffic lights as he passed through a village, and was about to slot an Elvis tape into the cassette player, when the chimes of an ice-cream van drifted through the air playing 'Just One Cornetto'. Eddie laughed and joined in, substituting Elvis's lyrics for the ice-cream jingle and continuing solo after the accompaniment had ended. It was his favourite Elvis ballad, and as he drove on to the northbound carriageway his voice soared over the roar of the traffic as he reached the finale: '*It's now or never! My love can't wait!*' He held the final note, one hand on the steering-wheel, reaching out to his audience with the other. Passing motorists cheered and waved. Eddie acknowledged them with a grin and blown kisses. He saw himself kneeling at the front of the stage, receiving a garland from an adoring female fan, then it was back from New York to the open road.

He was travelling behind a luxury coach with a London–Newcastle destination board in the back window. Eddie imagined that it was Elvis's tour bus and that he and Jet were following him round the country attending every concert on his nationwide tour. As Eddie pulled out and passed the coach, he looked up at the windows and saw Scotty Moore and Bill Black, Elvis's guitar and bass players, playing poker, and there was Colonel Tom Parker, Elvis's manager, reading *Record Mirror* and smoking a cigar . . . Then Elvis, sitting alone, staring out of the window across the bleached country-side. Eddie pointed up at the window.

'There he is, look,' he whispered, nudging Jet. 'The King.'

And the King looked down and winked at them as the Cadillac surged by. Eddie gave a 'Yahoo!' and slapped the car door.

'This is it kid! This is what we've been waiting for! Your choice! What do you want to hear?'

Jet selected an Elvis tape, fast-forwarded the first track, then waited in anticipation for the opening line of the next number.

Well, it's one for the money.

Eddie turned up the volume.

Two for the show.

He checked the mirrors.

Three to get ready. So go, cat, go!

He squeezed the accelerator and away they went, booming up the highway. Kings of the road.

But don't you step on my blue suede shoes.

The music sent shivers through him. He felt invincible, heroic. He was a racing driver, an astronaut, the pilot of a Flying Fortress taking off. He had never known such excitement and power. He could have conquered the world.

Blue, blue, blue suede shoes . . .

The heavy beat buffeting vehicles like a cross wind as they thundered by . . .

*

As soon as they had heard the record, Eddie and Jet went into town to buy some blue suede shoes, beetle-crusher style with thick crêpe soles. Jet quickly found a pair, but none of the shops had a size 11 in blue so Eddie had to settle for black, consoling himself with the thought that they would match his new black shirt and wouldn't show the dirt.

That night, they visited the Cats Eyes, a regular rock 'n' roll venue in the basement of a coffee bar. Everybody said they called it that because it was so dark that you needed cat's eyes in order to see anything. The only light was provided by candles stuck into Chianti bottles on the tables and the juke box in the corner. The regular joke amongst the customers was that if you made a date with somebody in the Cats Eyes, you never recognized them when you met them next time. Burt Lancaster turned into Boris Karloff overnight, and the boy who arranged to go to the pictures with Marilyn Monroe found himself sitting next to Old Mother Riley, hoping and praying that none of his mates would see him.

> *Blue, blue, blue suede shoes,*
> *You can do anything*
> *But stay off of my blue suede shoes.*

It was difficult to stay off anybody's shoes in the Cats Eyes it was so crowded. Eddie was wishing that he had put on his work boots. His new suedes had cost him half a week's wages and they were being ruined the first time on.

'Watch where you're treading!' he shouted, pushing a jiving youth back on to the dance floor.

Jet was jiving with a girl wearing a tight sweater and full skirt. Every time he twirled her round, her skirt flared out, revealing her suspenders and knickers. The next time he met Eddie, he would recount in lascivious detail what had happened in a shop doorway or up a dark alley on their way home. He made it sound so easy. According to him, they were always 'panting for it' or 'they couldn't get enough'. Eddie didn't know whether to believe him or not. It never worked out like that for him or for any of the other boys he knew. But you never knew with Jet. He was such a charmer with the girls that it might, just possibly, be true.

Eddie was eyeing up the talent sitting at the tables and standing around the dance floor with their friends. He was looking for someone to dance with when the next record came on. Then he saw her. She was standing by the juke box, lit by its neon glow, and when 'Blue Suede Shoes' ended and the next record fell, Eddie's heart fell with it. He had always thought that falling in love was something that only happened in soppy films and songs, but now, gazing across the room at the girl with the shining hair, the strings of his heart really did go zing.

'Do you want to dance?'

She looked him over. A brawny lad in a Teddy-boy suit with his hair set like concrete.

'No, thanks.'

'Why not?'

'I'm waiting for somebody.'

'They all say that.'

'It's true.'

It was – she was waiting for her girlfriend to come out of the toilet – but that wasn't the main reason; there were some brilliant dancers on the floor and she didn't want to be embarrassed by a lumbering ox.

'Come on! It's a great record this!'

He was shouting above Jerry Lee Lewis hammering out the piano chords on 'Johnny B. Goode'. She hesitated. It was one of her favourites too. Why not? He seemed pleasant enough in spite of his tough-guy looks, and if she led him into the middle of the floor, nobody would see them anyway.

'All right then.'

It was worth the acceptance just to see the look of pleasure on his face.

'What's your name?'

'Pearl.'

'That's nice. It sounds like a film star.'

But there was no leading him into the thicket of jiving couples. Eddie remained at the edge of the dance floor, where there was more space and they were in full view of the wallflowers.

Oh no! Pearl thought. Thank God the record's half over.

Eddie took her hand, waited for the beat – 1–2 – then twirled her round. They performed light, deft moves, with Eddie taking the lead. Pearl was amazed by his skill. She could see people admiring them from the side. Tarzan had turned into Fred Astaire! Eddie spun her faster and faster, her blonde hair flying loose. Jet waved to him from across the floor but Eddie pretended not to see him and looked away. *Johnny be good*, Jerry Lee advised as the record ended, leaving Eddie and Pearl smiling into each other's eyes.

'Phew!' Pearl said, panting as if she had run for a bus. 'That was great. You dance as if you've had lessons.'

He had. But he didn't tell her who from.

*

Eddie and Jet had been to see *Rock Around the Clock* at the Alhambra. They had swaggered out of the cinema full of bravado, ready to set the town on fire and Eddie was still restless and full of excitement when he arrived home and began to tell his mother about the film.

'. . . And when Bill Haley was playing this concert, all the kids in the audience jumped up and started jiving in the aisles. It was great . . .'

Stella was ironing in front of the fire. Eddie watched her deft manoeuvres around the collar and buttons of one of Jack's shirts.

'You should have seen 'em, Mum. I wish I could dance like that.'

Stella arranged the shirt on a coat hanger, then hooked it on to the picture rail.

'Push the sofa back.'

'What for?'

Stella took off her pinafore, then unpinned her hair and shook it loose.

'I'm going to teach you how to jive.'

'You what?'

She smiled into the overmantel mirror and smoothed down her skirt, as if she was making final preparations in a dance hall cloakroom.

Eddie watched her, panicking at the thought of dancing with his mother. It was too embarrassing to think about. It would be like taking her on a pub crawl or telling her a dirty joke.

'*You* can't jive.'

Eddie couldn't either but at least he knew what it looked like.

'We called it jitterbugging in my day. It's only the same thing. Go on, move the sofa back to make some space.'

She collapsed the ironing board and rolled up the hearth rug. Reluctantly, Eddie pushed back the sofa to the wall. At least Jack and his sisters weren't there to see him make a fool of himself.

'Put 'Rock Around The Clock' on, as you've just seen the picture.'

Eddie walked across to the record player on the sideboard and shook the record out of its sleeve. Stella was moving with the rhythm and miming the lyric even before the needle came down. Eddie couldn't believe that this was his mother. Suddenly, she had become a younger, different person.

'*One, two, three o'clock, four o'clock rock*,' she sang along with Bill Haley.

'Come on Eddie,' beckoning him.

He blushed as she placed one of his hands on her waist, then held the other one.

'I'll take the lead. Just react to my prompting and relax. You'll soon pick it up.'

She danced him slower than the music, but he didn't know where to place his feet. They wouldn't move. He was shod in lead boots. He was nailed to the lino.

But it wasn't just his clumsiness that embarrassed him, it was dancing with his mother, holding her hand and feeling her breasts against him as she pulled him towards her before spinning him round. He was aroused and repelled simultaneously.

They played the same record several times. Sometimes Stella forgot that Eddie was a novice and left him stranded after a turn or a spin. Then she would apologize and take him through the movements as if she was teaching him to waltz. But as the music continued through Danny and the Juniors and Chuck Berry, she became frustrated. It was another, more responsive hand she sought, swirling her away then gathering her back in. She closed her eyes and forgot about Eddie, leaving him embarrassed and sweating, watching her solo jive. He couldn't believe it. This was his *mother*, for Christ's sake! It was like one of those films in which the plain girl takes off her glasses and turns into a beauty queen. Only in this version, his mother takes off her pinafore and turns into a rock 'n' roll queen!

The record ended, but Stella continued to dance to the music inside her, winding down gradually like a clockwork doll. Then, when she opened her eyes and saw Eddie staring at her, she blushed.

'I think we'd better leave it there for tonight. We don't want to wake our Brenda and Carol up. And your dad'll be back soon.'

The threat of Jack's imminent return from the pub was usually enough to send him straight up to bed to avoid trouble. But not tonight. He wanted to know more.

'Where did you learn to dance like that?'

Stella kept her head down as she pulled the sofa away from the wall. She knew that Eddie was watching her, waiting.

'During the war. They used to have dances out at the American airbase —'

She broke off, sobbing, then put her arms around Eddie and held him close.

'Don't you blame me as well, Eddie, please. I've suffered enough as it is.'

*

Eddie pulled up in a lay-by, switched off Del Shannon singing 'Runaway' and threw away the tape. He lit a cigarette. The fields of ripe corn, pale gold in the sunlight, reminded him of the colour of Pearl's hair when she was young. Suddenly he missed her. He felt sick in his stomach. He was tempted to turn around and go home. He scanned his Elvis tapes for a sentimental ballad to match his mood, then settled back and wallowed in 'The Wonder Of You'.

She's been a good wife. None better. A good mother too. Brought the kids up a treat. He looked at his watch. Saw Pearl standing on the pedestrian crossing with children walking past her. Works her bollocks off. Three fucking jobs. Not as many as Jacko's wife, but it's still enough. They've got that many scams going between them in their house, that you need a calculator to add them up. One'd do me. Just one. That's enough for anybody. I must have been crazy buying this car. There's no wonder she gets fed up with me. She'll be wondering where I am. Perhaps not. Perhaps she's glad to see the back of me. Let's face it, I haven't done much for her lately. We haven't exactly been setting the bed on fire. And she's still attractive. She still looks smart when she's dressed up. I've seen 'em looking at her when she walks down the street. Dirty bastards. Especially Robbo. No wonder though, married to that foul-faced cunt. I'd sooner fuck a rat than fuck her. I'll kill the bastard the next time I see him. I'll give her a ring when I stop for a bite to eat. Stop her worrying. She'll start nagging though. As soon as she hears my voice she'll start nagging. But she might not. She might be worried. No, she won't. I know her. She won't care. Where are you? What are you playing at? That's all she'll say. I'll show her though. Nobody treats me like shit.

Going on about the car. Whose money is it anyway? I've worked hard enough for it, for fuck's sake. Nobody can accuse me of shirking. I've worked like a dog. Do us good, a break. A couple of days away. Give us time to think. Sort things out.

He had come too far to turn back. If he didn't make the journey now, he knew that he never would. He eased his way back into the traffic and cruised along in the inside lane, considering the past. What if Jet hadn't died? What if he hadn't married Pearl? What if Jack had followed up his inquiries and they'd emigrated to Australia to start a new life?

'One thing's for certain,' Eddie said, turning to Jet. 'We wouldn't be sitting here, kid.'

He maintained his reflective mood with a selection of Elvis ballads, joining the King on stage at the Las Vegas Hilton. Oblivious behind his shades, with his left hand reaching for the audience, the soldiers in the army truck in front thought he was singing to them and they applauded and cheered like an audience in the balcony. But Eddie neither saw them nor heard them until the last refrain had faded: '*You are always on my mind. You are always on my mind.*' Then he looked up, waved, and took a bow. 'More! More!' they yelled. So he played them 'Jailhouse Rock' at full volume and caused a riot in the back of the truck.

Watching the soldiers fooling around, suddenly reminded him of the expression 'passion wagons', the unofficial name for the trucks which ferried local girls out to the American airbase for Saturday night dances during the war. Eddie hated the expression, and in spite of all his mother's protestations, he used to imagine her lying in the back with Yankee airmen.

Eddie passed the truck then moved across to the outside lane and kicked down, eager to leave the memory behind him. But he couldn't drop it, however fast he drove. It hung on, niggling away and the memories became so oppressive that he checked his rear-view mirror to see if he was being pursued.

'It wasn't like that! It wasn't!'

His mother was sitting on the sofa, crying into her hands. Eddie was standing in front of her with a torn shirt and a bleeding nose.

'Why didn't you tell me? Why?'

'I was going to, love. I was going to. I was waiting till you were older and you'd understand better.'

She reached out towards him. Eddie, his face filthy with smeared tears, swung out at her with his fists. He was nine years old and, in the school playground, had just discovered who his real father was.

'What the fuck!'

The container lorry in the middle lane was veering right towards him. He couldn't brake because of the car on his tail and he couldn't accelerate clear because of a Transit van in front.

'Get over, you stupid bastard!'

But it kept coming, heading him off, edging him towards the barrier. He could have reached out and touched the monster wheels beside him. The crash barrier slid by, inches away on the passenger side of the car.

'Jesus! Jesus, fucking God!' he roared, waiting for the screech of tearing metal . . . But it didn't happen. They were still running dangerously close but he wasn't being forced over any more; then a widening gap appeared as the truck veered back into the middle lane. Eddie accelerated clear but his relief quickly gave way to rage and he waved his fist wildly as he glared into the rear-view mirror.

'You stupid bastard! What the fucking hell do you think you're playing at?'

He wiped the sweat from his eyes then shifted tentatively from buttock to buttock to check that he was still dry. *That* would have been a disaster, having left home without a spare pair of trousers and underpants. But he had survived without mishap and now that he was safe, and his heart was no longer trying to escape, he lit a cigarette and played out an escalating scenario of retribution.

First, he would drag him out of his cab and give him a good hiding. But that was too lenient, so he set the truck on fire. But even that wasn't enough. He deserved to die. In the burning truck. After receiving a good hiding. Working up to a flaming crescendo which required the attention of the police and medical and fire services. And a vicar to console his grieving wife. But it served her right anyway for marrying such a stupid cunt.

He moved into the middle lane and cruised along to the Platters to calm himself down.

'That was a close shave, kid,' he said, turning to the empty seat. 'I thought I was coming to join you then.'

Eddie was frowning through his sunglasses. He was done in. Too much to drink, followed by nightmarish sleep, a hangover and near-fatal crash, had caught up with him and he was relieved to see a road sign advertising a café a few miles ahead.

When he climbed out of the car, he stretched and yawned

so extravagantly that he staggered and almost fell. Feeling foolish and hoping nobody had seen him, he crossed the car park to the café, which turned out to be a converted caravan. Eddie studied the menu on the chalk board at the side of the serving hatch and ordered a triple-decker burger and a large Coke. The young woman behind the counter nodded past him and smiled.

'Nice car.'

'Yeah. Thanks.'

'I'd love a ride in a car like that.'

She laughed, revealing lipstick smeared teeth. The chef, frying burgers on a hotplate behind her, glanced round but remained silent. The woman studied Eddie's tattoos.

'It's like an art gallery.'

'Yeah. On tour.'

'I've always wanted a tattoo but Greg says they're common, don't you Greg?'

Greg turned round, revealing a Two Fat Slags cartoon on his damp T-shirt.

'Onions?'

Eddie nodded. 'Yeah, thanks.'

As the woman leaned forward and studied his arms, Eddie could see that she was wearing only a bra under her white overall. She pointed to the faded scroll on his bicep.

'An old flame?'

Eddie smiled and flexed the muscle.

'Yeah . . . My latest flame too.'

'What's her name – Marie?' the chef asked without turning round.

Eddie laughed and the waitress looked from one to the other, puzzled.

'What's the joke?'

They didn't tell her, and Eddie whistled the tune as he crossed the picnic area with his burger and Coke and sat at a table near his car.

'Litter louts,' he said, sweeping screwed-up crisp packets on to the grass. He bit into his burger and then lifted the sleeve of his T-shirt and examined his new tattoo. It looked inflamed and felt sore when he pressed it, and he regretted taking off the dressing straight away. Then, gently – far more gently than his latest tattoo – he touched the name on his bicep. It was his first tattoo and still his most precious. Jet had followed him into the chair and had *his* name inscribed in capital letters above a star.

Eddie watched people inspecting his car. They walked around it as if it was a tourist attraction, and some of the men had their photographs taken standing in front of it. One couple even had a row over it.

'It's brilliant!' the woman kept saying, smiling and shaking her head as she lapped the car, while her husband looked on in disgust.

'Brilliant? It's a monstrosity! It's the worst car I've ever seen!'

'Worse than ours?'

'What do you mean? What's wrong with our car?'

She ignored him and paused to read the front number plate.

'*And* personalized number plates. How stylish! I wonder who owns it?'

She looked across the picnic area, assuming Eddie, who was sitting at the nearest table, to be a truck driver.

'Just imagine, driving along the open road with the wind

in your hair, the sun in your face and loud music playing.'

She closed her eyes and inclined her face towards the sun.

'There's enough noise pollution as it is.'

'It's better than listening to that interminable cricket.'

'It's the finest game in the world, cricket. You don't understand it, that's all.'

'Who wants to?'

'And it must cost a bomb to run.'

She ran her hand lightly along the top of the door then gripped the chrome handle.

'Yes, but what a ride.'

A butterfly fluttered around her husband's head then tried to land on his shirt. He stepped back in a panic and tried to flap it away.

'Don't be cruel!'

To a heart that's true, Eddie sang to himself.

'It made me jump. I thought it was a wasp.'

'What, with red wings? It was attracted by your shirt. It thought you were a daisy.'

She blew herself a kiss in the wing mirror, then walked across the grass towards the caravan, followed by her husband. In his white shirt, dark trousers and polished shoes, he looked like an umpire going out to inspect the wicket before a match.

Eddie wiped his fingers on his serviette then stuffed it into his empty Coke carton. The food, and relaxing in the sunshine, had made him tired, and he was considering stretching out on the grass and taking a nap, when he noticed a silver truck pulling into the car park. Suddenly he was wide awake. He jumped up and hurried towards it, his anger building with every stride. Yes! That was the name of the company on the door! And yes! That was the bastard driver in the check shirt who had tried to kill him!

Eddie was waiting for him when he jumped down from the cab. As soon as he hit the ground, Eddie smashed him in the face. The driver slammed back against the front wheel. Eddie hit him again and he went down. Then he loured over him, waiting for him to get up so that he could hit him again. People were watching, but at a safe distance. Somebody said, 'Call the police.' But nobody did. They didn't fancy the prospect of Eddie turning round and catching them on the mobile.

During the time that the driver lay senseless on the oil-stained concrete, Eddie's anger subsided. He had exacted revenge and he was satisfied.

The driver sat up and leaned back against a wheel, feeling his face to assess the damage.

'What was that for?'

Eddie nearly kicked him for asking such a stupid question.

'What do you think, you stupid cunt? Back there! Trying to kill me!'

A man parked nearby, offended more by Eddie's language than his brutal attack on the hapless truck driver, ushered his wife and children back into their car.

'I don't know what you're talking about.'

He opened his mouth painfully and felt his teeth.

'It's a good job they're not false, or they'd be down your fucking throat, I can tell you.'

'I still don't know what I'm supposed to have done.'

Eddie felt like nutting him to remind him. He pulled the driver to his feet and pointed to his car.

'Remember that?'

The driver paused. Blood was dripping from his chin on to his shirt.

'The American job?'

'Yeah. The American job.'

'I remember it going past. You don't see many about. Why?'

'Why?' Eddie's anger flared up again. 'Because you tried to fucking kill me, that's why!' The driver narrowed his eyes at the gale-force roar. 'You tried to force me off the fucking road, you bastard!'

Customers, crossing the car park to the café, hurried nervously by the savage scene. The truck driver appeared to forget all about Eddie's threatening presence, even though he was being held up on his toes by the front of his screwed-up shirt. He just stared at the car then slowly shook his head.

'Sorry, mate.'

Eddie was so surprised by this unexpected apology, that he let the man go.

'You admit it then?'

'No. I didn't try to cut you up. I must have dozed off at the wheel. I'm knackered. Absolutely knackered.'

He took out a handkerchief and dabbed at his nose.

'Where are you heading for?'

'Dundee.'

'That's a fair way.'

'Yeah. Three or four hours at least. I've been on the road twelve hours already, and we're not supposed to drive more than ten hours a day.'

'Cost cutting, isn't it? It's the same everywhere.'

'And they don't care a fuck about safety. I came back from a job on the continent last week – Holland and Germany

– and drove for ten days without legal stops. I mean, I didn't run bent because I wanted to, I'd no choice if I wanted to keep my job. The wife and kids have forgotten what I look like. The last time I went home the fucking dog bit me. He didn't recognize me when I walked in!'

Eddie laughed and offered him a cigarette.

'At least you've got a job, even if it is shit.'

'Yeah.' He exhaled, then stared off to the side as if he was looking for something. 'The trouble is, it's either overwork or no work, with nothing in between.'

Eddie felt embarrassed as he watched the driver feeling his bruised nose.

'Sorry about the punch-up.'

'That wasn't a punch-up. It was an ambush.'

'Yeah. I do get a bit hot-headed at times, I must admit. You can imagine how I felt though. I thought my time was up, I can tell you.'

'I'll bet. It's the sort of thing some silly bastards do when they see a flash car. Jealousy, I suppose.'

'Anybody who's jealous of me must be in a bad way, I can tell you.'

They both laughed. Eddie nodded towards the caravan.

'Can I treat you to a burger or something?'

He looked away, embarrassed. He had never apologized for hitting anyone before.

'Forget it. I'll grab a quick cup of tea and then get on my way.'

'Well, make sure you give me a good start before you set off.'

They laughed and shook hands.

'See you, Eddie.'

Eddie stared at him, surprised.

'How do you know my name?'

The driver pointed at the back number plate of the Cadillac.

'It's pretty obvious, isn't it?'

Back on the road again, Eddie played 'His Latest Flame', and smiled at the chef's laconic reference to the record and the puzzled expression on his partner's face when they laughed. He imagined he was in a film. The woman has had a row with her boyfriend and walked out on him. He sees her hitching at the side of the road, picks her up and they roar away down the deserted highway, accompanied by a riotous soundtrack of rock 'n' roll. That was the film. In reality he was stuck behind a tractor on the busy A1, listening to a depressing ballad about a boy stealing his friend's sweetheart.

Eddie shook his head, still trying to convince himself. No, it wasn't like that. Jet didn't steal her from him. He had finished with her before Eddie and Pearl had even met. They hadn't even been going steady, but Eddie was still jealous of what might have happened between them. He was a smoothie was Jet, only interested in one thing. The girls knew it too, but it didn't stop them going out with him. Even Pearl, his beautiful Pearl, and it erupted occasionally throughout their marriage, usually when Eddie had been drinking . . .

'Nothing happened. How many more times do I have to tell you?'

'Of course it did. I knew what he was like.'

'He wasn't like that with me.'

'That's not what he said.'

'What did he say?'

'That you'd gone all the way.'

'Well, he was lying.'

'How far did you go then?'

'Christ almighty! Do you want the details?'

'No! I want the truth!'

'I've told you the truth!'

But he didn't believe her. He didn't believe Jet either. He never knew who to believe.

He passed a road sign for Scotch Corner, then a few miles further on, another one for Penrith, A66.

'Remember that, kid, when we used to study the map? We used to call it Route 66.' He shook his head and laughed. 'Let's see how many names we can remember . . . Scotch Corner.' He paused before supplying Jet's response: 'Penrith.'

Eddie: 'Carlisle.'

Jet: 'Gretna.'

Eddie: 'Annan.'

Jet: 'Dumfries.'

And so on, until finally, when Eddie called out the last town on their route, he cheered for both of them, delighted that he could still recall the names after so many years.

He thought about Pearl and looked at his watch. She would probably be in the supermarket now before going on crossing duty at the play scheme. When he thought about her earlier, she was large in his mind, a lifesize, overpowering presence. But now, hours later and distanced from home, her image was smaller, as if he was watching her on television. Was she thinking about him? Was she upset? Had she phoned the council about the hole in the wall? He felt bad about that. As if she didn't have enough on her hands already, without leaving her with that mess to sort out. Perhaps later on, he could phone the Greyhound and ask the landlord if he knew any brickies who would be glad of the work.

Eddie thought about the young soldiers in the back of the army truck and wondered how many of them would have joined up if they had been able to get a job. He wondered what would have happened if national service hadn't been abolished just before he was due to be called up, and he had gone away for two years. He might have gone abroad. Met another girl somewhere. Lived a totally different life . . . He remembered Jack, bitter and disillusioned after his life as a soldier.

'The army's the university of the working class,' he would declare, swaying in front of the fire after returning home from the pub. 'Gives you a broader perspective of life, and brings you into direct contact with the ruling class, the officers. And what a shower of shit they were, most of 'em. If they'd had gunpowder for brains, they wouldn't have had enough to blow their hats off.'

Eddie liked it best when he paused and went cross-eyed with concentration as he tried to light a cigarette.

'It was the returning servicemen won the 1945 general election, you know.' They knew. They knew it off by heart. 'They wanted something different after all that killing and sacrifice. They remembered the thirties and unemployment and they wanted decent housing and jobs. That's why they voted Labour, for a new start and a brighter future. They even postponed election day so that returning servicemen could vote. It didn't affect me though, did it?' Now was the time to watch out. 'I was rotting in the jungle in Burma, wasn't I, still fighting the Japs? The Forgotten War, that's what they called it. And they soon forgot about us when we got back!'

Then he would kick something. Or lash out. Usually at Eddie.

Eddie turned off the road and stopped in an open gateway leading into a field. He reached into the glove compartment and removed one of Jack's airmail letters from the photograph album. He tried to smooth it out on his knee, but the fold lines were so ingrained, that it closed protectively like a butterfly's wings.

Darling Stella – the endearment was so heartfelt and private that Eddie blushed and looked away for a few moments –

> *I'm writing this sitting by the camp fire. Just had our suppers – K rations as usual which just about keeps you going. How I long for a good Sunday dinner – roast beef and Yorkshire pud. Another days trek through the jungle under sniper fire from the Japs. Can't say any more about that though it's confidential. I think I've got a touch of malaria. I'm feeling a bit feverish, sweating and shivering and that. I've just taken a mepacrine tablet. That should clear it up. It's nothing compared to what happened the other day though. One poor lad, Ted Flowers a cockney lad copped it when a load of rations fell on him from an American parachute drop. Poor bugger. Can you imagine, he'd survived the Japs, malaria, dysentery, heatstroke, mosquitos and leeches and then to be killed like that. If that's not bad luck I don't know what is. I think the authorities should cover it up myself and tell his parents*

*that he was killed in action. At least they'd think his
sacrifice had been worth while. I'm running out of paper
so I'll just finish by telling you how much I love you and
the only thing that keeps me going in this rotten hole is
thinking about you and how great it's going to be when I
get home. I can't wait. I miss you so much. When we're
marching through the jungle I just concentrate on the back
of the man in front watching his pack and whistling that
song 'Stella By Starlight' over and over again. In fact
some of the blokes have threatened to shoot me if I don't
shut up. They say it's worse than the Chinese water torture.
I'm going to get into my sleeping bag when I've finished
this letter. But before I go to sleep I'll take your photo out
of my tunic jacket like I do every night and whisper I love
you and good night.*

Eddie wiped his eyes on the back of his hand then blew
his nose over the side of the car. He imagined himself in
Jack's position, sitting round the camp fire in the jungle,
dreaming of home. Darling Pearl . . . He could feel it for
him. Counting the days. Wondering if he would ever see
her again. Wondering if he would ever return to a normal
life.

But eventually, after the VE-Day and VJ-Day celebrations
had passed, Jack arrived home one drizzly November
evening. He hurried down the street in his cheap demob suit
with his kitbag over his shoulder. There were no buntings
or street parties to greet him, but he didn't care. He was
home! Home at last after four harrowing years. What would
Stella look like? Would she still be as beautiful? Would she

still love him? Would she even *recognize* him? Bouts of malaria had left him much thinner than when he went away. He felt like Stan Laurel wearing Oliver Hardy's suit.

There it was! And there was a light in the living room. She was in! His stomach turned with nervous excitement. She wouldn't be expecting him. What a surprise it would be! He had sent his last letter three weeks ago, before they had set sail, but there was no guarantee that she would have received it, and even if she had, he hadn't been able to specify a definite date of arrival.

He opened the front gate then walked down the path. He could hear music from inside: 'In The Mood' by Glenn Miller. He grinned. He was definitely in the mood. When he had finished his supper, they would sit by the fire and play 'Stella By Starlight' on the gramophone and he would tell her about the war and then . . . He laughed. He still couldn't believe it. He was home! This was his house. His wife was waiting for him inside. This was the start of their new life.

He swung his kitbag off his shoulder and grasped the door handle. Then he paused and grinned. He would give her a real surprise! He released the handle and rapped a jaunty little solo on the door. After a pause, the kitchen light went on and a blurred figure appeared behind the frosted glass door panel. Jack's heart was beating too fast. He couldn't catch his breath. He thought he was going to die of excitement. He had survived four years of jungle warfare only to expire on his own doorstep.

The door opened and there she was, Stella. His lovely, beautiful, wonderful, Stella. Suddenly he felt shy. He didn't know what to say; what to do. Stella just stood there, staring at this strange man. Then her hands went up to her mouth and she shouted, 'Jack!' He rushed into her arms and hugged her as if he would never let her go.

'Stella,' he kept saying. 'Oh, Stella. I've missed you. I've missed you. I've missed you.'

She started to sob and he felt her tears on his cheek.

'Don't cry. It's all over now. We're back together again and that's all that matters.'

Still smiling, he opened his eyes and, looking over Stella's shoulder, he saw a little boy standing in the hall doorway staring across the kitchen at him.

Poor bugger, Eddie thought, putting himself in Jack's place. By the time you're grown up yourself and understand these things it's often too late.

Suddenly there was a bellowing chorus behind him which made him spin round in terror.

'What the fuck!' he roared, when he saw the cows with their heads straining over the boot of the car. His shout frightened them and they tried to back off, but they were trapped by the rest of the herd, trying to turn into the field from the road. Eddie had a horrifying vision of the cows stampeding over the car, leaving him plastered to the seat. One cow managed to squeeze between the car and the gatepost, mooing into his face as it scraped by. Fearing for the paintwork, Eddie started the car and accelerated across the field, followed by a stampede. He didn't know much about the behaviour of cattle. He wasn't sure if they would turn vicious and charge and he would have to fight them off like Victor Mature in *Demetrius and the Gladiators*. So in order to keep them at bay, he slid a tape into the player, turned it to full volume and suddenly the fields were alive with the sound of Bill Haley. Unimpressed, they swished their tails and eyed the car warily before lowering their heads to the parched grass.

'Hey you! What the bloody hell do you think you're playing at?'

Eddie slipped on his wraparounds and waited for the farmer to approach.

'Sorry, pardner!' Eddie shouted as he loomed over him. 'Ah was just doin' a spot of map reading back there, being kinda lost an' all, when suddenly I'm ambushed by a bunch of steers! Sure gave me one helluva fright, I can tell you!'

The bogus accent checked the farmer for a moment and he stared at Eddie through the rock 'n' roll hurricane with narrowed eyes.

'You've no right to park in that gateway! It's private property! You're trespassing!'

Eddie screwed up his face and cupped his hand behind his ear.

'Sorry, pardner! I can't hear you!'

'I said! I said, you've –'

Eddie switched off the tape mid-sentence but the farmer was already launched and it was too late to throttle back. His voice was so loud in the ensuing silence that he scared a magpie out of a tree and the cows raised their heads from grazing.

'Hell! I didn't have much choice with a whole bunch of steers comin' up behind me. I had to move mighty fast back there or my car might a been scrap metal.'

Eddie had to concentrate hard on his rôle to stop himself

from laughing at the farmer's clothes. He was wearing an old cap with a peak so greasy that it reflected the sunlight, and the state of his shirt and trousers made Eddie wonder if he earned a few bob on the side as a scarecrow.

How he wished that Jet was with him now, the two of them when they were teenagers, facing the apoplectic farmer in his shit-caked wellingtons. They would break into a double act. Sometimes they were American singers called the Jones Boys on their way to perform at the Palladium in London. Eddie argued that the Brooks Brothers – modelled on the Everley Brothers – was a much slicker name, but he never got his way. At other times, they were a couple of American servicemen on leave looking for a good time, or they were working for Elvis, checking out the venues for a forthcoming European tour. But whichever story they chose, they could never finish it. At some point one of them would catch the other's eye and they would start laughing, which in turn gave the game away and resulted in the girls whom they were trying to impress snatching up their handbags and flouncing off.

Eddie had to stop staring at the farmer's swashbuckling, turned-over wellingtons or he would have gone into solo hysterics.

'Perty little herd of cattle you've got here, sir.' If he had been wearing a hat, he would have tipped it back. 'I keep a few myself back home. Let me see now, I must have seven, eight, maybe ten thousand head of longhorn, I guess.' Eddie was John Wayne now at the beginning of the cattle drive in *Rio Bravo*. 'It's mighty different to the bitty little fields you have over here of course. My land stretches as far as the eye can see.' Behind his monologue, Eddie was singing 'Home on the Range'. He could see the deer and the antelope roaming with the steers. 'Why, my property is so huge, I can drive for hours before I reach my boundary fence.'

The farmer didn't look impressed. Wearing a Boddingtons T-shirt and his arms swarming with tattoos, Eddie didn't look much like a beef baron. Unless he was like that Howard Hughes chap he had read about who was worth billions but dressed like a tramp. Eddie didn't like the way the farmer was stabbing at the ground with his stick. It was time to leave before he was rumbled.

'Ah'm over here on vacation, travelling up to Scotland trying to discover mah roots. Ah'm a member of the McBrooks clan. Eddie McBrooks is mah name.' He thought of Jet and had to work hard to prevent himself from laughing. 'We were driven from our rightful land by the English way back in the eighteenth century.'

He knew about this episode in Scottish history from watching the film *Bonnie Prince Charlie*. The farmer nodded, eager to see Eddie depart from *his* rightful land as soon as possible. Usually, he was able to terrify intruders with a shout and a wave of his stick, but this one was different, he wasn't scared.

'I'd better mosey along, as we say back home. Hope ah haven't caused you any trouble now.'

'No, not at all,' the farmer said, looking for a revolver in the glove compartment as Eddie replaced the photograph album and Jack's letter.

He followed the car as Eddie bumped slowly back across the field then went ahead and opened the gate for him.

'Thank you kindly, sir.'

'No problem,' the farmer said, proving he was no hayseed.

'Have a nice day.'

Eddie turned into the road then raised his arm and pointed ahead. 'Take 'em to Missouri, Matt!' he roared, as he accelerated away.

With the frantic A1 behind him, Eddie relaxed as he headed across high country towards Penrith. A patchwork of fields fell away from the road and sheep, grazing under the high sun, sought the thin shadow of the walls.

'"Top o' the world, Ma!"' Eddie shouted, as he topped a blind summit and dipped down the other side. But Jimmy Cagney's defiant cry reminded him of his own mother and he lapsed into melancholy. What a hard life she had led, especially the early years after the war. Eddie could never understand why Jack was so cruel to her, and why he couldn't sleep with his mother any more and had to sleep in the cold back bedroom. He would listen to him shouting and cursing when he returned from the pub, and his mother crying 'No, Jack! Please, Jack! No!' Then he would hide under the blankets, dreading the footsteps on the stairs and the door bursting open.

But he understood now that he was grown up and knew the full story. He wondered how he would have reacted if he had returned home after four years of jungle warfare to find a bastard waiting for him. The same as Jack, he supposed. Worse probably, knowing his temper. And the birth of his daughters was no consolation. He wanted a son, his own son, to tell war stories to and take to football matches. Eddie ached for him to hold his hand like he held his sisters' hands when they went out, and when his mother tried to take it instead, he would pull it away angrily.

Sometimes, after work, when he had finished his meal, Jack would sit staring into the fire with a mug of tea, repeatedly whistling the same tune. He was back in the jungle then, crouched round the camp fire after a harrowing day's march under sniper fire. Eddie would edge close to him, stealthily, imperceptibly, like a cowed dog seeking the double comfort of warmth and love. He wanted to share his dad's experiences. What was he thinking as he stared into the glowing coals? Sometimes, to no one in particular, he would relive a story from the war. There was the incident when he stopped a charging Jap with a grenade, then finished him off with his bayonet. And the time when his best mate Buck had his head sliced off during an ambush. Then, much to Eddie's frustration, Brenda and Carol would spoil it by starting to cry at the gruesome parts, and Jack would stop and stare at them, then blink his way back to the present.

Sometimes, Eddie was woken up by Jack's nightmares in the adjoining bedroom. The first time he heard him, he thought he was insulting his mother again, and he lay trembling in the dark waiting for the door to crash open and to be dragged out of bed. But what he was shouting didn't make sense – 'Over there! No! No! Get down!' – followed by his mother's soothing tones, and Jack sobbing and repeating, 'Stella, Stella, Stella,' over and over again.

But Eddie didn't feel sorry for him. Eddie was on the side of the Japs for most of the time and wished they had killed Jack in Burma.

Eddie discovered that Jack wasn't his real father in the playground at junior school. A gang of boys were arguing about who were the bravest fighters during the war. Some said submarine crews, others pilots and tank commanders. Their preferences were usually determined by the rôles their fathers and uncles had played during the war, spiced with film and American comic-book heroes. Then Eddie spoiled it by saying that kamikaze pilots were the bravest, because they knew they were going to die before they took off, and nobody could be braver than that. This took some thinking about and they all went quiet. But Michael Palmer was having none of it. His father had flown in Lancaster bombers over Germany and been awarded the DFM.

'That's stupid, committing suicide.'

Eddie shook his head.

'They did it for their country. The Japs were fanatics, my dad says. They used to pull the pins out of hand grenades and fall on them rather than be captured.'

'That's stupid an' all!'

But Roy Groves was impressed.

'That's brave. I once got hit with a cricket ball in the belly and it nearly killed me.'

Some of the others were impressed too and nodded their agreement. Encouraged by their interest, Eddie continued.

'And they'd throw themselves on barbed wire fences even though they knew they'd get shot, so that the others could climb over their bodies to attack the British soldiers.'

The boys stared at him, enthralled by the reckless heroics of the Japanese troops. It was like the climax of a western, when the Indians were mown down as they attacked the fort.

Eddie was enjoying being the main attraction, and he hurried on while he still held their attention.

'My dad says that the Japs used to shoot the mules sometimes when they were trekking through the jungle, and they'd fall down the bank with all their equipment strapped to their backs. And once my dad killed a Jap in the jungle. He said he jumped out at him and was just going to fire his rifle, when my dad threw a grenade at him then finished him off with his bayonet.'

Eddie stepped forward and demonstrated the thrust. The others boys clutched their stomachs and groaned. All except Michael Palmer. Nobody was going to displace *his* father as the greatest war hero and he was the one who made the killing thrust.

'He's not your dad.'

Eddie stared at him, left arm and leg still outstretched.

'Who isn't?'

'Your dad! He's not your real dad anyway!'

'What is he then?'

'Your dad's a Yank. Your mother used to go out to the airbase at Wharncliffe and go with the airmen.'

'Liar! You're a liar! You're just saying it!'

'I'm not! It's true! They called her a Yankee bag and a Yankee groundsheet! My mam says! Everybody knows!'

Eddie threw himself at him and wrestled him to the ground. Michael tried to struggle free but Eddie had him on his back with his arms pinned to the floor.

'You're a liar! You're a liar!' Eddie screamed, thumping him on the nose. 'My dad fought in Burma against the Japs!'

Michael struggled and started to cry, but Eddie sat tight and continued to pummel him. The encircling gang of boys looked on excitedly. They had never seen so much blood before and they moaned with pleasure at the sight of Michael spitting out a tooth on to the asphalt.

Suddenly, as if he had remembered an urgent appointment,

Eddie jumped up and ran out of the playground. He never saw the car which swerved on to the pavement to avoid him, or the dog which tried to ambush him as he ran across the estate. His mother dropped a cup into the sink when he banged into the kitchen, but her shock gave way to alarm when she spun round and saw Eddie standing in the doorway, panting and sobbing and his face filthy with smeared tears and blood.

'What's the matter, love? What's happened?'

Before she could move towards him, he ran across the kitchen and threw his arms around her.

'It's Michael Palmer!'

Stella patted his back to try to calm him down.

'Why, what's happened? What's he done?'

'He said my dad isn't my real dad! He said that he's a Yank from the airbase! He's not! He's not! He's not, is he, Mam?'

He sobbed uncontrollably into Stella's damp pinafore, while she held him to her and tearfully stroked his hair.

Eddie was too involved with the past to notice that the green and golden landscape had given way to the purple haze of moorland. He had hated them all at times: his mother, his absent father and Jack. Poor old Jack. He was the one who had probably suffered most and Eddie was sorry that he had never been able to make it up with him before he died.

He remembered visiting the war memorial outside the town hall with his mother and Jack on VJ-Day, in honour of his comrades who had died in the Far East. He even remembered the date, 19 August. Then, with a jolt, he remembered another date in August! A vital, momentous, far more important date as far as Eddie was concerned. The death of his mother, followed by his domestic crisis, had driven it from his mind. Her funeral had been on the third, or was it the fourth? He had signed on last week. No, it was the week before. What date was that? He couldn't remember, but he knew that it must be close. He would never forgive himself if he had forgotten it.

He pressed on the accelerator and rumbled across the high moors, desperate to reach a village or a town where he could buy a newspaper. But he couldn't wait. He wanted to know immediately, and when he approached a young man trudging along the side of the road with his thumb out, Eddie slowed down and pulled up beside him.

'What date is it?'

'What?'

'The date! What date is it?'

The hitch-hiker hesitated, confused. It was the weirdest opener he had ever heard. It was usually a straightforward 'Where you going?' He looked Eddie over: a big, heavy-looking dude with a prehistoric haircut. He didn't look like the sort you'd want to tangle with, even though he was getting on a bit. Perhaps he was a weirdo, a serial killer who stopped people in lonely places, and if they didn't answer the question correctly, he blew them away, then stuffed the body in the boot of his car. Such things did happen. It happened all the time in America. He had read about it in the *Daily Sport*.

'What you staring at?'

Eddie glared at him impatiently. Just his luck. The first person he had seen for miles and he turns out to be a village idiot. It was due to all that inbreeding out in the country. He had read about it in the *Daily Sport*.

The hitch-hiker considered making a run for it across the moors, but the heather was deep and dense and he imagined both barrels of a hidden shotgun in his back before he had gone ten yards.

'It's the sixteenth of August.'

'Are you sure?'

'I'm positive. I'm due in court today.'

He produced his summons from his jacket pocket to prove it. Eddie breathed out deeply and smiled with relief.

'Good.'

Eddie's apparent levity annoyed the hitch-hiker and his anger overcame his fear.

'It might be for you. But it's not good for me, I can tell you.'

'It's nothing to do with you. Do you know what day this is, the sixteenth of August?'

The hitch-hiker looked back along the road hoping to see another vehicle approaching. All he wanted was a lift into town, not an audition for *University Challenge*.

'Well, I'll tell you, seeing as you're so bloody ignorant. It's the anniversary of Elvis's death. He died on the sixteenth of August 1977 at Graceland.'

The sun twinkled on the hitch-hiker's earring and Eddie took it as a sign from the King that he had been pardoned for his transgression.

'It's a sacred day this, kid,' Eddie said, releasing the handbrake and shifting into drive. 'It should be on the calendar like Christmas and Easter.'

'I'm not old enough to remember.'

'You're not old enough to remember the death of Jesus but you still know about it, don't you?'

Eddie looked into the rear-view mirror and prepared to

move off. Realizing that he was in danger of being left behind, the hitch-hiker stepped close to the car.

'Aren't you giving me a lift?'

Eddie stared at him, his thoughts elsewhere.

'Yeah. OK. Where you going?'

'Mayfield.'

'Where's that?'

'Just a couple of miles down the road.'

'OK. Jump in.'

As the hitch-hiker walked round the car and opened the door, a volley of gunfire echoed across the moor.

'Hear that? It's a twelve-gun salute to Elvis.'

The hitch-hiker shook his head.

'It's not. It's a shooting party. The grouse-shooting seasons's just started.'

They drove along the moorland road to the intermittent crack of gunfire in the distance. The hitch-hiker gave it a two-fingered salute.

'I tried to get a job beating, but they said they didn't need anybody else.'

'No wonder, with a haircut like that,' Eddie said, scanning the hitch-hiker's green Mohican. 'They probably thought you'd turn up with a bow and arrow and shoot all the grouse.'

The hitch-hiker smiled to keep on the right side of him.

'You sound like my dad.'

'What are you up for?'

'Shoplifting.'

'What did you nick?'

'Some booze and some curling tongs.'

Eddie laughed. 'Curling tongs? For *that*!'

The hitch-hiker looked offended.

'Not for me. For my girlfriend. It was a birthday present.'

It didn't seem like much of a birthday present to Eddie, but it beat the pork chops he once took home for Pearl.

'What time are you in court?'

'Two o'clock.'

Eddie looked at his watch and gave a low whistle.

'You'd better have a good excuse.'

'I know. I couldn't get a lift.'

I'm not surprised, dressed like that, Eddie thought, noticing the boy's kneecaps protruding through his ripped jeans. But he kept his sarcasm to himself. The lad was in enough trouble as it was.

'Isn't there a bus into town?'

'Yes. But I've no money.'

At intervals, the few grouse which had survived the barrage flew low across the road and glided to safety in the deep heather. Every time they appeared, the hitch-hiker leaned forward expectantly.

'If you hit one, stop the car. I'll be able to sell it.'

But Eddie wasn't listening. Watching the grouse take cover in the heather reminded him of the time he had taken Pearl to the pictures to see a war film. In the final scene, a shattered Flying Fortress with an engine on fire, a dead navigator on board, and riddled with holes from German anti-aircraft fire, struggles home across the Channel. Back at the airfield, the pilot's girlfriend tearfully searches the sky waiting for the return of her sweetheart . . .

And the tears started to roll down Eddie's cheeks too, just like they had forty years ago, sitting in the back row of the stalls with Pearl. A tough guy, dressed to kill in his Teddy-boy suit, with tears dripping on to his Slim Jim tie. That pilot was his father, his real father, and the girlfriend was his mother. And when the plane pancaked in and slewed across the runway, and the fire crew just managed to get his father out of the cockpit before the plane blew up, and his mother ran towards him and they embraced, Eddie began to cry openly with his shoulders shaking. Pearl was sweating with embarrassment and the people sitting round them sniggered and stared when the lights went up . . .

Unlike the boy in the Alhambra, who finished up unconscious amongst the tab ends and ice-cream wrappers, the hitch-hiker had the good sense to look away. Eddie wiped his cheeks with the back of his hand.

'I've got a bit of a cold. Makes my eyes run.'

The hitch-hiker sniffled in solidarity, pointedly admiring the dials on the dashboard.

'Yeah. It's a bug that's going round.'

They entered the outskirts of Mayfield, drove past the cattle market with its empty pens and sheds, then turned into the busy High Street.

'Where do you want dropping off?'

'Anywhere'll do.'

He got out at a red traffic light before an audience of curious pedestrians and envious drivers.

'Thanks mate. I appreciate it.'

'Forget it. All the best in court.'

'Yeah. Depends on which magistrate I get.'

The traffic light was still at orange when the driver directly behind Eddie papped his horn. Eddie ignored him.

'Is there a clothes shop round here?'

The hitch-hiker turned round, surprised.

'Yeah.' He pointed along the road. 'There's Bailey's just

past the town hall. Sells country gear. You know, check shirts and sports jackets, that sort of thing.'

'What about casual stuff, jeans and that?'

The traffic light had changed to green, but the driver behind Eddie left his horn untouched, even though drivers in the queue behind him were sounding off. He didn't like the look of the heavy in the American job. Even from the back.

'There's Babylon, just past Boots up there. That's the best place.'

'Thanks.'

'See you.'

The hitch-hiker hurried off, amused at the thought of Eddie striding along in a hacking jacket and brogues.

Eddie continued along the High Street, then, as he turned into the market square, the driver following him felt safe enough to risk a sustained blast of the horn, followed by a two-fingered salute. Eddie parked near the fountain in the middle of the square, closed the hood and windows then got out of the car and stretched noisily. He was tired. It seemed more like days than hours since he had left home. He promised himself a rest in a lay-by when he had completed his business in town.

A pair of pigeons landed on the marble lip of the fountain and dipped their beaks into the brimming water. Eddie turned to a farmer, who was standing next to a dust-covered pick-up truck in a nearby parking space.

'Is that water drinkable?'

'Well, it's not killing them pigeons, is it?'

It's a good job Little Benny's not here, Eddie thought, or *he* would be. He'd have them necked, plucked and sold in twenty minutes. He could see the farmer examining his car with peevish eyes.

'Bastard,' Eddie said, loud enough for the farmer to hear him. Since the steelworks had closed, he had worked for short spells as a driver, as a security guard and on building sites, but worst of all, and for the lowest wages, he'd done seasonal agricultural work. Kids in Kashmir weaving carpets get more than this, he used to complain at the end of a back-breaking day picking peas in rain-sodden fields.

He was tempted to throw the farmer into the fountain just for the hell of it, but he didn't like the look of the shit-caked sheepdog in the back of the pick-up. Sneaky buggers, sheep-dogs. It might sneak up and bite his ankle just as he was heaving its master into the water. Cupping his hands, he had a long drink at the cool jet arcing from the cherub's mouth then, after wiping his hands on his jeans, he produced a wad of notes from his hip pocket and asked the farmer if he could change a fifty for the parking meter. The farmer was too surprised to reply, but the dog perked up at the sight of Eddie, then watched him keenly as he walked away, laughing.

As Eddie strolled along the High Street, a cloud passed across the sun, draining the colour from the hanging baskets outside the shops and the flower tubs spaced out along the pavements, and making people instinctively glance up. Eddie stopped outside a travel agent's and looked in the window at the list of bargain flights and posters of exotic holiday resorts. Perhaps that's what they should do when he returned home. Take a holiday. Somewhere sunny where they could relax and spend some time together. Talk things over. They never seemed to talk about anything these days. All they did was argue and sulk.

He went inside and came out with a stack of holiday brochures for countries worldwide. The pictures of suntanned beauties stretched out on sun loungers, and smiling couples enjoying candlelit dinners in elegant clothes excited him, and he looked forward to phoning Pearl to tell her about his plans. The sun came out again, which enhanced his mood, and he was whistling 'Burning Love' when he entered Boots.

He walked down the aisle between Family Health and Haircare to the pharmacy at the back of the shop and, while waiting to be served, examined the range of pregnancy kits on the counter.

'Can I help you, sir?'

Eddie looked up. The assistant looked like one of the blonde beauties on the holiday brochures. She expected Eddie to look embarrassed and quickly replace the box. Instead, he said,

'How do they work?'

That knocked the smirk off her face. She took the kit from Eddie and went into customer service mode.

'Well, there are different kinds –'

Eddie laughed and shook his head.

'Forget it. At least that's one thing I don't have to worry about any more.'

Somebody had once told him that women became more randy after their menopause, but it didn't seem to have worked with Pearl. He lifted up the sleeve of his T-shirt and revealed his new tattoo.

'I've just had it done and it's a bit sore. Have you got anything to soothe it?'

The assistant stared at the number. Eddie could see that

she was dying to ask him what it meant. He saved her the trouble.

'It's my prison number. It's an advanced form of electronic tagging. They implant electrodes under the skin.'

The assistant tried to smile but it wouldn't stay put. Eddie bought a jar of Vaseline for old times' sake. His mother had always used it to soothe his cuts and grazes and Pearl had continued the practice with Danny and Jane.

'Do you know where a shop called Babylon is?'

'Yes. It's just along the street, past the Ship Inn.'

Eddie noticed her staring at the wad of notes when he paid for the Vaseline.

'Don't worry, I didn't kill the guard. I'm an innocent man.'

'It's a mark of respect!' Eddie roared at the bemused assistant over the thunderous music, as he tried on a black T-shirt, size XL, in the middle of the shop. He decided to keep it on, and outside, as he was stuffing his old T-shirt into his back pocket, he saw the hitch-hiker across the road.

'Hey!' Eddie shouted and waved, and a puzzled stranger, thinking that Eddie was shouting at him, waved back. Dodging the slow-moving traffic, the hitch-hiker nipped across the road.

'They haven't banged you up then?'

'No. They've adjourned it. I've to come back next month.'

'What for?'

'I was too late. By the time I arrived, the magistrate had gone home.'

Eddie laughed. It could turn into a serial.

'It's no joke. I've come all that way for nothing.'

Eddie took out his wad and peeled off a dud tenner.

'Here. Get the bus home.'

The hitch-hiker hesitated then took the note.

'Thanks. That's great. Thanks.'

'Forget it. And keep out of trouble. You'll save a fortune in shoe leather.'

Eddie gave him a parting slap on the shoulder which almost knocked him under the wheels of a passing tractor. He left the hitch-hiker standing on the pavement, then, on a hunch, looked round just in time to see him disappearing into the Ship Inn.

The farmer had disappeared too from the market square and a Reliant Robin had taken his parking space next to the Cadillac. Eddie laughed. They looked ridiculous together: the Batman and Robin of motor cars. Eddie walked round his car to check that the farmer hadn't spitefully scratched the paintwork with his stick, or allowed his dog to piss on the wheels and stain the white-wall tyres. But there was no damage and he unlocked the door and slid inside. He reached forward to release the hood then changed his mind. He wanted to remember the day that Elvis died, in private . . .

He was at work. 'Elvis's dead!' somebody shouted above the roar of the furnace. He couldn't believe it! Elvis dead? It was impossible! A sick joke. Another wind-up from one of the lads. But it was true all right, and all that evening the television companies rescheduled their programmes and screened hastily assembled biographies of Elvis's life.

Eddie vaguely remembered the death of King George VI some time in the fifties. But he was a distant figure who had made no impact on his life. But the death of Elvis was different. This time the *real* King was dead. It was a true occasion for national mourning. After watching early tributes on television, Eddie went down to the Greyhound and jammed the juke box with Elvis records until long after closing time.

Before resuming his journey, Eddie smeared Vaseline on the inflamed skin around his tattoo, then selected a tape of Elvis ballads to commemorate the anniversary of his death. He was aiming for a sombre, dignified mood, like on Remembrance Day, when Jack used to pin on his medals and take part in the ex-servicemen's march through town.

As he left Mayfield in a long, halting line of traffic, Eddie pretended that he was part of the cortège at Elvis's funeral. The squeegee merchant, working his pitch at the traffic lights before the dual carriageway, spoiled the dignity of the occasion somewhat, but how was he to understand the significance of the cavalcade? Some of the drivers in front weren't as sympathetic though. Eddie could see them shouting and cursing him when they stopped at the lights. Eddie couldn't understand how the boy stood for it. If he had been on the receiving end of such abuse, they would have finished up with the bucket through the windscreen.

The traffic began to move again and Eddie was second in line when the lights changed back to red. The driver in front refused to have his windscreen washed, so the boy moved swiftly to Eddie.

'Wow! What an ace car! First time I've done one of these.'

As he manoeuvred the squeegee deftly across the glass, Eddie noticed that he was singing along word perfect to 'Crying In The Chapel' on the Elvis tape.

'Do you like Elvis?'

'Yeah. I know every number.'

'All of them?'

'Yeah. Off by heart. My mother's an Elvis freak. I was brought up on him.'

'Do you know what day it is today?'

The boy flicked water off his squeegee on to the grass verge.

'Yeah, sixteenth of August. It's the anniversary of Elvis's death.'

Eddie laughed, and shook his head.

'You should be on *Mastermind*.'

'Ask me anything. I'm an encyclopedia of Elvisology.'

The lights changed, followed by an immediate fusillade of hooting from behind.

'Do you know, "An American Triology"?'

'Yeah. Sure.'

'Go on then, sing it.'

The boy paused. Soapy rivulets wobbled down the windscreen

'What, here?'

'Yeah. Why not?'

The boy looked away and laughed.

'You must be joking.'

'Not when it comes to Elvis, lad.'

The boy looked around. He didn't know what to say. He pointed his squeegee at the line of traffic stretching back into town.

'What about this lot? They'll lynch me.'

'Don't worry about them. That's my department.'

'I don't know.'

'What's the matter, can't you sing?'

That stung.

'Of course I can sing!'

'Come on then, let's hear you. Your mother'll be proud of you.'

'Yeah. Pity she's not here. She'd join in.'

'There you are then.'

The boy held up his bucket.

'I'm losing a lot of trade you know.'

'Don't worry. It'll be taken care of.'

The boy looked at Eddie, looked at the car. It was a weird set up but he believed him.

'Well, it'll be something to tell my mates. Not that they'll believe me.'

He put down his bucket and squeegee beside the car then climbed up the grass verge. A driver several vehicles back leaned out of his car window and screamed abuse. Eddie got out and sized him up. The apoplectic driver turned apologetic and hurriedly closed the window even though it was baking inside. Eddie noticed that the driver in the Audi directly behind him was using his mobile. Eddie strolled back to him and bent down.

'I hope you're not doing anything stupid like phoning the police.'

'No, no,' panicking and pushing down the ariel. 'I'm just phoning the wife.'

'Tell her to pop your dinner in the oven. You'll be a bit late.'

Eddie walked back to his car and got in.

'I'll play you in, OK?'

The boy waited before the hostile, captive audience while

Eddie fast forwarded the tape. Then he heard the guitar introduction, followed by Elvis:

> *Oh I wish I was in a land of cotton*
> *Old times there are not forgotten . . .*

Eddie turned up the volume, and as Elvis's voice soared over the countryside, the boy joined in . . .

> *Look away. Look Away.*
> *Look away, Dixieland.*

Eddie gradually reduced the volume during the chorus until the boy was singing solo.

> *In Dixieland I'll take my stand*
> *To live and die in Dixie.*

And he too had a rich, clear voice which carried down the line of traffic and silenced the impatient travellers.

> *For Dixieland's where I was born,*
> *Early Lord one frosty morn.*
> *Look away! look away!*
> *Look away, Dixieland.*

They were listening now, and those who were too far back to hear clearly, strained out of their windows trying to work out what was happening ahead.

> *So hush little baby, don't you cry*

And the traffic travelling in the opposite direction seemed to hush a little too as it passed by.

> *You know your daddy's bound to die*
> *But all my trials will soon be over.*

There were tearful eyes in many vehicles and Eddie was blinking as if he was travelling through a storm. Then, at the opening of the second chorus – *Glory, glory hallelujah* – the audience joined in – *Glory, glory hallelujah* – and it travelled down the line of traffic – *Glory, glory hallelujah* – working towards the climax – *His truth is marching on! His truth is marching on!*

'Yes!' Eddie shouted, wiping his eyes. 'Encore! Sing it again, kid!'

The boy was willing, and the audience were keen to hear an encore too, and the spirit of Elvis was relayed from lorries to vans, to motor bikes, and cars: all the way back into town, where the hitch-hiker, light-headed after a quick couple of pints, thought he was suffering from the DTs when he emerged from the Ship Inn to discover the High Street alive with 'Dixie'.

Back at the traffic lights, there was emotional applause for the boy when he finished his song. Eddie jumped out of his car and nearly crushed him with a hug.

'Well done, kid! You've done the King proud!'

He gave the boy a ten-pound note then threw the water out of his bucket.

'Here. Hold that out when they come past. You'll make a fortune.'

And drivers, who a few minutes earlier would have gladly run him down, rattled his bucket with silver as they crept by.

Eddie played the track again, but quietly, in a sentimental mood as he cruised along in the inside lane. He was playing it for Jet, who had died before Elvis had recorded the song.

It had been a sorry time for rockers. First Jet, then Buddy Holly, killed in an air crash, closely followed by Eddie Cochran. Eddie had tapes of both singers in the car and he included them in his Elvis Memorial Service as a mark of respect.

Love is strange, Buddy Holly sang as Eddie passed a road sign for Gretna and Dumfries. He had never been to Scotland before. When they were planning their route on the map, Eddie used to imagine taking Pearl along with them and getting married at Gretna Green. They would be in all the papers, like Jerry Lee Lewis and his teenage bride.

It all came back as he entered the town and saw the signpost for the blacksmith's shop where eloping couples used to get married. He imagined them standing arm in arm by the anvil, and the blacksmith in his leather apron conducting the service with a bible in his hands. The fire glowed in the gloomy interior and a carthorse stood witness in the background.

Why did couples get married in the blacksmith's shop? Weren't there any churches or registry offices in Gretna? Still, it wasn't as odd as getting married in bed like Matt Jackson, who played in the darts team at the Greyhound. He had got so drunk on his stag night, that he was too ill to get up the following morning. It looked as if they would have to postpone the wedding, but the bride wasn't going to let him get away with it as easily as that, so she climbed into bed with him, fully dressed in her bridal gown, and the vicar conducted the ceremony standing in front of the wardrobe, with the guests spilling out on to the landing.

Eddie considered stopping and buying Pearl a souvenir. There would be plenty of gift shops selling lucky heather and miniature malts, and newly weds in snow storms. But he decided against it. He felt uneasy in a town dedicated to marriage when he was on the run from one.

What to do now that she doesn't want me? Buddy sang.

'Fuck knows,' Eddie replied as he headed out into open country towards Dumfries.

He looked at his watch. When he had set out that morning, he hadn't worked out the mileage or how long it would take him to reach his destination. His main concern had been getting away before Pearl returned. It was time to make plans. He pulled up at the side of the road, spread out his map across the steering-wheel and calculated how long it would take. Yes, he could make it in the day then travel back overnight. But what was the rush? He was hardly going to receive a hero's welcome when he arrived home.

He decided that his best plan would be to stay overnight somewhere close by, then travel the last few miles in the morning, refreshed after a good night's sleep. After replacing the map in the glove compartment, he paused and gazed across the fields. But he didn't notice the cattle raise their heads at a sudden wind, or heavy clouds piling up behind the distant mountains. How painful it had been, having a father whom he never knew. If only there had been one letter or photograph to make him real. Sometimes, when he was alone in the house, he would search his mother's bedroom. He ignored the obvious places like the dressing-table and chest of drawers because he figured that Jack would have had the same idea and already searched them. If there was any correspondence, it would be hidden in a secret place and Eddie would crawl about the floor pulling back the lino, or pressing the flowers on the wallpaper hoping to find a concealed cupboard. He never dreamed of looking anywhere else in the house. He was playing out scenes from films he had seen, where romantic intrigue always took place in luxurious bedrooms with silk sheets and tiger-skin rugs. He had never seen Bette Davis open a love letter in the coal cellar.

After a beating, when he used to lie in bed plotting revenge, the cruellest punishment he could invent for Jack was hoping that he would find a love letter from his father in his mother's knickers drawer.

How he had longed to see a photograph of his father, or touch his handwriting and trace his finger over his signature at the end of a letter. He used to question his mother about him when she was gay and relaxed after jiving sessions on the hearthrug. Briefly, it brought the three of them together.

'What did he look like?'

She lay back in the armchair, eyes closed, chest heaving. He had to wait before she could answer.

'I've told you a thousand times.'

But Eddie wanted to hear it for the thousand and first.

'He was tall with dark hair. Your colouring.'

Eddie was always thrilled when she said that. The rest of the family were mousy. On holiday snaps, Eddie looked as if he had wandered in from a different family.

'He said he'd got Red Indian blood in him, but I never knew whether to believe him or not.'

Eddie was thrilled at the notion. It meant that he had Red Indian blood in him too. No wonder he had become a good dancer with ancestors like that. He was glad that he didn't take after Jack – weedy little fucker. *He* looked as if he had descended from a ferret.

'He was nice and ever so polite. The Yanks had this

reputation for being big mouths and throwing their money around, but they weren't all like that. I liked Ray the minute I saw him.'

The three American airmen bought their tickets then walked across the mirrored foyer examining their change.

'What's this one?'

'That's half a crown.'

'So which one's the crown?'

'There isn't one. Just half.'

'So where did the other half get to?'

They laughed, then turned their attention to Stella as she tore their tickets by the potted palm at the inner doors. She blushed at their extravagant flattery and thrilled at being called 'baby', 'honey', and 'doll'. They looked like film stars in their tailored uniforms and she thought of Jack in his rough khaki and how it had scratched her cheek when he kissed her goodbye.

'What's the movie like?' the boy with the dark eyes and Tyrone Power looks asked.

'I don't know. I haven't seen it yet. When it's loosing, the customers say it's good.'

'Loosing? What the hell does that mean?'

'Loosing. Coming out.'

'Loosing.' Tyrone Power shook his head and laughed. 'When are you guys going to learn to speak English?'

They pushed through the double doors into the auditorium, releasing a blast of gibberish from Donald Duck and leaving behind a sweet smell of deodorant. It was as if a group of WAAF's had entered the cinema, rather than airmen.

139

During the interval, as Stella stood before the curtained screen with an ice-cream tray round her neck, Tyrone Power walked down the aisle and bought three choc ices.

'Hey! You look like a star, standing there in the spotlight. You should be up there on the screen.'

A gang of ragamuffins, sitting on the front row of the chicken run, jeered and banged their seats, and a cross-eyed boy wearing wire-rimmed specs yelled, 'Got any gum, chum?'

Tyrone Power pointed at him with a choc ice and the silver paper sparkled like a firework in the spotlight.

'You watch your mouth boy or I'll whip your ass!'

That shut him up. It shut up the rest of them too. But as they sat there, waiting for the lights to dim and the big picture to begin, they tried to puzzle out what the Yank meant. Whip his ass? Specky hadn't got an ass. He hadn't even got a dog to whip, never mind an ass!

'Take no notice of them, sugar.'

'I don't. There's no harm in them.'

'What's your name?'

'Stella.'

'That's nice. Stella by spotlight, eh?'

'Yes. I suppose so.'

She wished he would sit down now. A queue had formed behind him and she was convinced that everybody in the audience was watching them. Some people knew her. She could hear the rumours already. A married woman, her husband fighting overseas and there she was flirting with this Yank. She could hear the tut-tutting spreading like the beat of tom-toms all over town.

'Hey! Ray!' One of the airmen was on his feet, half way

up the stalls. 'Are you buying ice-cream, or making the damn stuff?'

There was laughter from the audience and people in the balcony stood up and tried to see what was happening downstairs.

'Bloody Yanks,' a man in the queue grumbled as Ray walked back up the aisle. 'They think they own the bloody world.'

The following week, Ray returned to the Alhambra on his own and invited Stella to a dance at the airbase. Flustered and blushing, she refused, then told Mr Ronson the manager that she felt ill, and went home in case Ray asked her again on the way out and she succumbed.

But she regretted it, even though she knew that she had made the right decision. She found herself looking for him. Every time the heavy glass doors swung open, she hoped that he would appear and smile at her across the foyer.

But as the days passed, she gave up hope and took refuge in righteous indignation. What does he think I am anyway? He must have seen my wedding ring. They're all the same them Yanks with their loud mouths and sweet talk. I bet he's tried it on with lots of girls. They all do. They're only interested in one thing.

Then he returned. But not at the door at the beginning of the programme, but magically, unexpectedly, walking down the aisle towards her as she stood in the spotlight at the front of the stage. Stella thought she was going to swoon, and in a state of total confusion, served a boy an orange-flavoured ice lolly instead of raspberry.

'Hi! How you doing?'

Instead of disguising her feelings with a cynical put-down, like Mae West, she replied, 'Fine thank you' and blushed fit to match her scarlet uniform.

Before she left the house, Stella took off her wedding ring and tried to assuage her conscience by wearing it on another finger, but the incriminating groove in her soft flesh made her feel even more guilty. She hid it behind the clock on the mantelpiece, then put on her coat and hurried out. She kept threatening to turn back. It wasn't right. She was a married woman with a husband fighting abroad. But it was harmless. She had to have some fun while she was still young. Once Jack came home, they would be starting a family and that would be it. And she hadn't been to a dance for ages. She used to go to the Roxy regularly when she was single, but Jack wasn't keen on dancing. Perhaps he wouldn't mind, the Americans being our allies and that. She was ashamed of her duplicity, but it didn't stop her running when she saw the bus approaching.

As the bus left the estate behind and continued the short journey into town, Stella left Jack behind too and became excited and nervous at the thought of meeting Ray. It was like her first date all over again. She got off the bus at the market and joined the group of girls waiting for the truck to take them out to the American airbase. They were boasting to each other how gorgeous their new boyfriends were and comparing presents they had received. One girl dabbed perfume on her neck, then walked around with her chin up inviting complimentary sniffs, and a bold, blonde girl raised her skirt to her bare thigh to show off her new nylons.

Stella, convinced that passers-by would recognize her,

stood in the shadows under the awning of a market stall, wishing that the truck would hurry up. How she envied the other girls. They weren't hiding away. They were single and free, looking forward to a good night out with their Yankee boyfriends. They knew it wouldn't last, but what the hell, they were determined to make the most of it.

Stella was relieved when the covered truck came round the corner and contributed a silent cheer to the raucous welcome of the other girls. The noise unfortunately attracted the attention of a gang of local youths entering a pub across the road. They began to whistle and jeer and Stella had never felt so ashamed in all her life, when one of them yelled 'You Yankee bag!' as she was being helped up into the back of the truck.

They sat squashed together on two benches facing inwards, and Stella began to relax when they left town and drove out into the countryside, with the girls singing and swaying in time to popular swing numbers. The open arch at the back of the truck framed a full moon, and Stella took out her compact and angled the mirror to catch its reflection as she powdered her face.

Ray was waiting for her when the truck arrived at the airbase. He helped her down and squeezed her hand.

'Hi. Glad you could make it.'

Stella smiled but did not reply. She wasn't sure whether she was glad or not. She looked across the airfield where an aeroplane was standing at the head of the runway, its star insignia on the fuselage clearly visible in the moonlight.

'I've never seen a plane close up before. You never realize how big they are when they're in the sky.'

'Too darn big, I can tell you, when you're under fire.

You feel like a sitting duck at the fair. Sure is a fine aeroplane though, dies mighty hard, I can tell you.'

Until now, Stella hadn't thought about the airbase or wondered about Ray's job. It had all seemed vague and disconnected from her life, even when she heard the planes droning overhead as she lay in bed thinking about Jack. But now she was here, and could see aeroplanes and Jeeps and hear American voices, it all became real. Ray became a real person too, with a family and a job back home and probably a sweetheart as well. This reassured her. Tonight was just fun, an innocent night out.

'OK. Let's go.'

As they walked towards the brassy blare of swing music coming from the hangar, Stella remembered what Ray had said about being a sitting duck.

'What do you do here? You know, what's your job?'

'I'm a pilot.' He glanced round at the Flying Fortress on the runway. 'You know, the big birds.'

Stella tingled all over. A pilot! In love stories and films, the pilot was always the hero, the one who had the pick of the girls. And Ray had picked her! She thought of him in town with his friends, going round the pubs and dance halls sweet talking all the girls. Yet even after she had refused him, he had returned and asked her again. When she walked into the crowded hangar accompanied by Ray, with the trumpet section on their feet playing 'American Patrol', it was like a fanfare and Stella had never felt so special in her life. She was the Belle of the Ball. The star in the Big Picture.

'Would you like a drink?'

'Sure.' (She was a film star already.)

They stood in front of a trestle table sipping bourbon and watching the dancers. Ray introduced her to his friends, who shook her hand and flattered her with outrageous compliments. She was compared to Betty Gable, Rita Hayworth and Dorothy Lamour before she had finished her drink. She was a pin-up girl. Hollywood beckoned.

'Would you care to dance?'

Stella replaced her glass on the table and stepped out on to the floor with Ray. She had met Jack at a dance. He had come in with a gang after the pubs had closed, full of beery bravado. They stood at the edge of the dance floor teasing and daring each other to dance. Finally, when the last waltz was announced, Jack approached her and they shuffled around under the glittering revolving ball suspended from the ceiling. Away from his mates, he was pleasant and didn't try to maul her, and when he asked her out she agreed. But he wasn't keen on dancing and when they started courting, they only visited the Roxy if Stella suggested it.

But this was different. The atmosphere was vibrant and glamorous, with pretty girls dancing with handsome men in uniforms. And there was no shuffling around with Ray. He knew the steps. They waltzed formally, did the foxtrot, and when the band broke into 'In The Mood', Stella raised her arms, expecting a quickstep.

'Can you jitterbug? You know, jive?'

Stella had seen American couples jiving on the newsreels at the Alhambra but she had never tried it herself.

'I don't know. I've never tried.'

'Come on! I'll show you!'

Ray held her round the waist, caught the rhythm, then twirled her round and back again.

'OK, baby! Let's go!'

And go they did, with Ray taking the lead, twirling her round and drawing her back in. Stella quickly learned the basic steps and began to improvise: a fast double spin, a slow revolving shimmy, with Ray standing back, clapping in time. They were naturals together, anticipating each other's moves, and as the number reached its climax they turned back to back, locked elbows and Ray ducked, pulling Stella over his back and she landed cleanly without missing a beat.

There were appreciative whistles and yells from the side-lines, and when the band stopped playing and Ray lifted her off her feet and whirled her round in exhilaration, she had never felt so happy and free in all her life.

'Hey! That was fantastic! Ginger Rogers had better watch out!'

Stella smiled at him, pushing back strands of damp hair from her face.

'That was great. Thank you.'

As they turned to leave the floor, the lights dimmed and the band eased into a slow, romantic number. Ray took Stella's hand again.

'Remember this?'

Stella listened then shook her head.

'Not really.'

'Stella by spotlight at the movies when you were selling ice-cream. Remember now?'

Stella nodded and laughed.

'God, I was so embarrassed. There was a queue a mile long.'

'This is your song. Let's dance.'

Ray held her close, and as she rested her cheek against

his chest, she wished the band would play 'Stella By Starlight' for ever.

As Eddie resumed his journey north, he remembered how desperately he had wanted to become a pilot like his father, but the only plane he ever handled was in woodwork at school. He checked the fuel gauge. It was time to fill up again.

He drove for miles along a lonely country road, passing through remote villages, and he was running on empty and facing a long walk when he finally saw a petrol sign ahead. As he pulled up in front of the pumps, he saw a police car standing on the forecourt, then thought no more about it as he unscrewed the fuel cap. He felt so relieved when he saw the digits turning over, that he thanked God for his deliverance by whistling 'Three Steps to Heaven'.

Two police officers and the attendant glanced at Eddie as he walked into the shop. The young woman leaning on the counter and crying into her handkerchief didn't look up. The sergeant had his notebook out and Eddie assumed that she had been caught shoplifting.

'I was only here a minute,' the woman sobbed.

So what? Eddie thought, taking down a copy of *Penthouse* from the magazine rack. Some of the villains who hawked nicked gear round the Greyhound could clear B & Q in that time. He replaced the magazine, picked up a couple of pork pies and a can of Coke, then walked across to the counter. The sergeant stepped aside and nodded towards the window.

'It's a grand car you've got there.'

His growling 'r' reminded Eddie of Tony the Tiger on the old Rice Crispies advert.

'What kind is it?'

'It's a 55 Cadillac Eldorado.'

The young constable walked across to the window and stared out on to the forecourt, stroking his moustache.

'I'd give my left bollock for a car like that.'

'Constable! Language! I'd like to remind you there's a lady present.'

The constable spun round, embarrassed.

'Sorry, sergeant. Sorry, miss. I got carried away.'

Eddie was impressed by their good manners. They didn't treat shoplifters like that when they caught them in the precinct at home.

Eddie and the sergeant joined the constable at the window. Standing between them, he looked as if he was under arrest.

'They don't build them like that these days,' the sergeant said, shaking his head. 'I mean, how many of today's models'll still be on the road in forty years' time?'

The attendant's view of the car was restricted by the three men at the window, so he joined the line-up, leaving the weeping woman alone by the counter.

'It must be heavy on gas though. You've got to have a shilling or two to own a car like that.'

The cops gave Eddie a sidelong shufty and he was relieved when the attendant drew their attention back to the car.

'It looks a picture, standing there by the pumps. It's like a scene on that American series on TV.'

Sergeant: '*Dallas?*'

The attendant shook his head.

Eddie: '*Dynasty?*'

'I never watched it.'

Constable: '*Miami Vice?*'

'No. Not that one.'

They were stuck then and they stared at the crimson Cadillac, thinking hard. The constable stroked his moustache as he pondered. If it had been a cat it would have purred. The attendant offered them a Polo mint then replaced the packet in his monogrammed shirt pocket.

'Perhaps it wasn't a series. It might have been an advert –'

Before they could pursue this new line of inquiry, the tearful young woman banged her fist on the counter.

'Never mind his car! What about mine?'

What happened next was just like a film running backwards. The attendant hurried back behind his desk. The woman resumed weeping and the police officers assumed their former positions beside her. If Eddie had crossed to the door, the scene would have looked exactly the same as when he walked in.

'We'll just finish taking your details, miss.'

'You've taken them already! I've told you! I filled up my car. Came in to pay. And when I went out, it was gone! That's it. There's nothing more to tell, except that whoever's stolen it will be miles away by now.'

'Are you sure you didn't see anybody?'

'I've told you. No!'

'Calm down, miss. We're doing everything we can.'

Eddie caught the constable looking down her blouse as she leaned forward, sobbing. Whatever he saw made his moustache quiver. Eddie fancied a quick look himself but he was too far away. He turned and stared across the boggy landscape to distract himself. It was difficult to imagine how it had happened. How anybody could have remained unseen over such flat ground. Perhaps a weary jogger had succumbed to temptation, or an escaped prisoner hiding amongst the sheep had seized his chance. Eddie was imagining one of his Cheyenne ancestors slithering unseen over the tussocky terrain, when he was brought back to the present by the distant, but strengthening siren of a police car. Moments later, a hearse sped by with a flower-bedecked coffin in the back, followed by a Daimler carrying a dark blur of mourners. When the pursuing police car appeared in a frenzy of sirens and flashing lights, the mystery was complete.

The police officers at the filling station immediately forgot about their present case, and without a word of apology or reassurance to the young woman, they dashed outside and roared away in support of their colleagues to investigate the much more interesting case of the Mystery of the Flying Hearse.

'Bastards!' the distressed victim yelled, banging on the window. 'What about me?'

Eddie was glad to see the back of them. He distrusted the police even when they were being polite. It was just another tactic as far as he was concerned. Before the funeral chase had intervened, he was becoming increasingly uneasy about the interest the cops were taking in his car. Out of a combination of envy and spite, and using it as a means of delaying the irksome task of finding the young woman's vehicle, they might have worked round to asking him to see his driving licence, where he had come from, destination, and so on. There had been reports of recent thefts of vintage American automobiles, they would have lied. However, what he feared most was the thought of being asked to empty his pockets and reveal his wad of bank notes with its heavy bias of duds. It was time to leave before they returned.

The young woman opened the refrigerator and selected a Diet Coke.

'We should swap,' Eddie said, patting his stomach and indicating his standard Coke on the counter. He checked his petrol and refreshment bill on the till, then pointed to the young woman's can.

'Include that as well.'

'Thank you!'

And when she smiled and held his look, he felt that same sweet surge of pleasure as when he had first met Pearl.

He took out his wad – if that didn't impress her nothing would – and ostentatiously peeled off four tens. Disgruntled by the sight of such riches, the attendant held up the notes to the light and snapped them peevishly. Eddie enjoyed his disappointment. He would never have dreamed of passing counterfeit money with the law liable to return.

When the attendant handed him his change, he held up a ten-pence piece then pretended to bite it. The young woman laughed. Eddie picked up his Coke and pork pies.

'Can I give you a lift anywhere?'

She paused and then shook her head.

'No, thanks. I'd better stay here and wait for the police to come back.'

'I wouldn't bank on it. They'll be nearly at John O'Groats by now.'

She laughed again, looking him frankly in the eyes. He felt his heart flutter. It wasn't lust, like he felt when he flicked through a sex magazine or when he fantasized about the young women in the Greyhound as he tried to rouse his indifferent wife. It was more tender than that. It was the way he used to feel when he was courting Pearl, that feeling of nervous excitement when the bus stopped and she waved to him through the window.

Eddie opened the car door and slid on to the hot leather seat. He slipped a Jerry Lee Lewis tape into the player, hoping that the glamour of his automobile, plus rock 'n' roll, would prove irresistible and change the young woman's mind. But even Jerry Lee's razzle and wild piano riffs couldn't entice her and, reluctantly, he released the handbrake and pulled away. As he left the forecourt, he looked back. The young woman waved to him through the window. Just like Pearl.

Fool! he berated himself, trying to justify his disappointment. How could she come with him when she had to wait for the police to come back? But what really bugged him was the knowledge that she still wouldn't have accepted a lift, even if the police had told her to go home and they would get in touch later.

He continued the row with himself. And who can blame her? Would you have accepted a lift from you, if you'd been her? He imagined her telling the story to her boyfriend later.

'There was this big fat guy in the filling station with this huge American car. He bought me a Coke and asked if I wanted a lift. There was no way I was going to travel with him, even though it was a great car.'

'Dirty old git,' Eddie muttered.

'Who said that?' he shouted, looking round furiously at the back seat. He shook his head and laughed at himself for getting so worked up over such a fleeting encounter. He chose a selection of ballads and cruised along in a mellow mood, but ruefully he kept thinking about the girl. It would have been exciting bombing along with her beside him, with the wind in her hair, her skirt up round her thighs, '*And love in her heart for me,*' he said, remembering the line from a song which Jack used to whistle monotonously as he pottered around the house, cleaning his shoes or sitting at the table, filling in the football coupon after he had finished his tea.

He thought about the girl again. They were driving through a town, crawling along in dense traffic, with frequent stops allowing the locals a good gawp. And they'd look at him. And they'd look at her. And they'd look at the car. And the men would be so jealous that they would want to kill him.

Fat chance, Eddie thought. It only happened in stories and it was always the handsome young stud who did the pulling. He shook his head. He had to admit it. He wasn't handsome. He wasn't young. And he was certainly no stud. He was fat, fifty-five and fucked. His pulling prospects were strictly limited. He played Little Richard and cheered up when he heard 'Good Golly Miss Molly' and 'Long Tall Sally'. Two good old girls. He was back with his own age group again.

When he saw the police cars and the funeral party parked at the side of the road, he slowed down to try to see what was happening as he drove by. He was hoping to see the police officers covering men in dark suits with their legs apart and hands resting on the hearse. Instead, he saw men in dark suits protesting to the police officers, and a man in a kilt comforting a woman wearing a black veil and gloves who was sobbing into a handkerchief.

Eddie gave the two officers from the filling station a toot on the horn as he drove by. The young one was stroking his moustache as he listened to the indignant mourners. Eddie was disappointed that it wasn't a bust after all, but he tried to maintain the fiction by imagining gangsters heading for a pay-off, with a coffin stuffed with drugs or bank notes. But it always ended in farce when he thought of the gangster in a kilt.

But what was the true story? Why was a hearse travelling at a hundred miles an hour along a country road? It made no sense. It was a mystery of sorts.

He thought of Jet's funeral, standing crying at the grave side with his arm around Pearl, and Jet's mother sobbing into her handkerchief like the mourner at the arrested cortège which he had just passed along the road. He didn't cry at Jack's funeral though, a few years later. Even though he was old enough to understand Jack's behaviour towards him after returning from the war, he still couldn't forgive him for his blighted childhood. His mother had cried. He was surprised how badly affected she had been, especially as Jack had shown her such little affection. He had never seen him kiss her, or laugh and fool around together like the parents of some of his friends. Perhaps she wasn't crying for Jack after all. Perhaps she was crying for Ray, her lost, true love. Or for him, their son, who had borne the brunt of her folly.

First Jet, then Jack and now his mother. And what about Ray? What had become of him? Eddie remembered the time his mother told him that he was dead too.

'You don't know! You can't prove it!'

'Stop shouting, Eddie. The girls'll hear you upstairs.'

'I don't care! He's not their dad!'

Eddie pulled on his jacket, then snatched up the comb from the mantelpiece and combed his hair so fiercely that it crackled like an electric storm. Through the mirror, he could see his mother staring into the fire and biting her bottom lip.

*

She was hurrying along the roadside towards the American airbase, past a continuous line of vehicles travelling in the opposite direction. Airmen whistled and called out to her from Jeeps and trucks, but she took no notice. They were leaving! They were going away! She started to run but was soon gasping and out of breath. Don't go, Don't go. Don't go, she repeated to herself, in time with her thumping heart.

By the time she reached the airbase, she was stumbling and couldn't speak. The MP on duty at the gatehouse was so concerned by her condition, that he invited her inside to sit down. She shook her head and clung to the link-wire fence, gazing through at the airfield. The runway was deserted and gangs of rookies were collapsing the sleeping tents.

'Can I help you, miss?'

He had seen it all before, but rarely at this pitch. This broad was an academy award winner.

Stella turned round, rummaging in her handbag for her handkerchief.

'I'm looking for Ray. Ray Wallis.'

'Captain Wallis?'

'Yes. Is he here?'

'Hold on a minute.'

He disappeared into the gatehouse. Stella could have wept with relief. She thought he was going to phone him on the base. Moments later, the MP emerged, drumming his fingers on an envelope.

'He said you might call by. He told me to give you this.'

Stella stared at her name on the envelope, underlined emphatically twice. Then she took it from him and tried to remain calm as she removed the sheet of notepaper.

She read the letter many times before finally raising

her head and looking towards the hangar, where swallows swooped in and out through the open doors.

'Do you know where he's gone?'

'I'm afraid I can't reveal that, miss. It's classified information.'

'But how can I find him?'

'Sorry, miss. I can't help you there.'

'There must be some way.'

'Maybe he'll write.'

But how could he? She had never given him her address.

Sometimes, as she stood at the back of the stalls, with her ice-cream tray, waiting for the interval, there would be an item on the newsreel showing American aircraft on bombing raids over Germany.

'Come back,' she would whisper, shining her torch at the screen like a guiding light. 'Please, please, come back.'

'He's not dead! He's not!' Eddie shouted, throwing his comb at the wall. It bounced off and nearly fell into the goldfish bowl on the sideboard.

'He'd have got in touch, Eddie.'

'How could he when he didn't know your address?'

'He'd have found me. I know he would.'

'You're living in a dream world. You don't know what happened to him. He could have survived and gone back to America, for all you know.'

Stella shook her head.

'He'd have got in touch.'

'Why should he when you were married?'

She daren't tell Eddie her secret wish: that Jack would

die a war hero in Burma, then, after a decent period of mourning, she would marry Ray and set sail for America.

Eddie snatched up his jacket from the armchair and yanked it on, then picked up the comb and stabbed it into his top pocket.

'Where are you going?'

'Out!'

'Where to?'

'Mind your own business!'

'Eddie. Please. Haven't I suffered enough?'

He relented when he saw her staring forlornly into the fire, squeezing her hands between her knees.

'I'm going to the pictures with Pearl.'

'Be careful, Eddie.'

'What do you mean?'

'You know.'

'I'm not daft, you know.'

'I've heard that before.'

They were lying in the sweet meadow-grass by the perimeter fence, listening to the strains of 'Moonlight Serenade' drifting across the airfield from the hangar.

'No, Ray. No,' she whispered, staying his hand on her thigh.

He kissed her neck and exposed breasts.

'Don't worry, honey. Everything'll be just fine.'

'Wait a minute, Eddie.'

Stella walked across to the sideboard and took out a stack of old records. Eddie double-checked the time on his watch and the mantelpiece clock.

'I've got to go. I'm late.'

Stella sorted through the records then smiled as she read the label of the one she was searching for. She tipped it from its torn sleeve and carefully wiped the worn surface with the hem of her frock.

'What is it?'

'"In The Mood". It was the first record that me and your dad jived to; jitterbugging, he called it. I'd never done it before. I soon picked it up though. He was a good dancer, was your dad.'

Eddie stared at the record. Heard the familiar tune and saw his mother jiving with a GI. He had shiny black hair and fleshy lips. She was dancing with Elvis in *GI Blues*.

'Did he look like Elvis?'

'Who?'

'My dad.'

Stella laughed.

'No. He looked like you.'

She lifted the lid of the record player and took the record from him.

'Come on. Let's dance.'

'I can't. I've got to go.'

'Come on. In memory of your dad.'

'He's not dead.'

'He doesn't have to be dead to remember him.'

She switched on the record player and the automatic arm rose stiffly from its rest then swung out over the record. Stella took Eddie's right hand and he placed his left hand on her waist. They stood poised, waiting for the needle to cross the smooth, silent, rim. Then straight in with the horns. Stella closed her eyes. She was back at the airbase on a hot summer's night, and it was Ray who was holding her hand and spinning her round, not Eddie. 'Go, baby! Go!' Pulling her close and stomping cheek to cheek in a world of their own on the crowded dance floor.

Suddenly, the band stopped playing, leaving Stella floundering at the end of a turn. She opened her eyes, but it wasn't Ray she saw in his glamorous uniform. It was Jack, standing by the record player in his greasy boilersuit, his face flushed with drink.

'You bag!'

'It's only a bit of fun, Jack!'

'Yeah! I know your fun. That's where that bastard came from,' he said, jabbing his finger at Eddie. 'You and your fucking Yanks!'

He stared round, wildly bent on destruction. The record player was the nearest thing to hand, so he ripped off the arm and threw it across the room.

'You know what they call women like you, don't you?'

Eddie remembered the playground fight when Michael Palmer had insulted his mother.

'It's a long time since, Jack. Please, can't you let it drop?'

Stella sank down on to the sofa and covered her face with her hands. Jack stood over her, kneading his fists by his side.

'Let it drop! How can I, when I see that bastard every day?'

'Don't blame him Jack. It's not fair.'

'Fair! *Fair!*' He glared about the room again. Eddie knew what was going to happen next. 'And was it fair while I was fighting in that stinking jungle, you were laying with your legs open under them Yanks?'

He could no longer restrain himself, and he smacked Stella

across the head, sending her sprawling across the cushions. Eddie grabbed Jack by the shoulder and spun him round.

'Leave her alone!'

Jack stared at him. His eyes were as pink as a white rabbit's and Eddie could smell the beer on his breath.

'What did you say?'

He couldn't believe what Eddie had just done.

'You heard. Leave her alone.'

Jack swung a blow at him, but Eddie stepped back and caught Jack's fist in his palm, like a baseball. Jack struggled to free himself and they staggered around the room, banging into furniture and spilling water from the goldfish bowl, when they crashed into the sideboard. But Eddie, fuelled by years of pent-up hatred, gradually wrestled Jack to a standstill and pushed him up against the wall.

'Had enough?'

Jack looked away to one side, gasping for breath. Eddie released him and stepped back.

'Listen. If you lay a finger on my mother again, I'll kill you! Understand?'

Jack still wasn't looking at him. Stella stood up and touched Eddie's sleeve.

'That's enough now, Eddie.'

She righted a chair and sat Jack down at the table.

'Would you like a bit of supper?'

She placed her hand on his shoulder. Jack stared at the rumpled tablecloth then put his hand over hers and began to cry. Eddie left the room, embarrassed and angry with both of them.

In the hallway, Brenda and Carol were sitting on the stairs with their arms around each other, looking terrified.

'You two! Get back upstairs!'

They scuttled back up to the landing, looking even more terrified when he slammed out of the house, shaking the windows and shattering the glass panel in the door.

The flatlands had given way to a sombre landscape with shadows sweeping across the hills. Eddie passed a woman and a little boy picking blackberries from a hedgerow. When they turned round and waved, he was surprised to see that the woman was Asian.

It'll be some old sheep-shagger; brought her back from Thailand he thought, watching them through the rear-view mirror and waving back. Poor cow, stuck out here in the wilds with some old tosser with a broody hen under his hat. It wasn't much of a life to travel ten thousand miles for. But she looked happy enough, and he thought about the life that Wurzel had rescued her from. She was better off here picking blackberries than being picked up at a couple of quid a time in a bar in Bangkok. Anyway, who was he to be criticizing anybody's marriage, considering the way that his had turned out? The journey from Thailand made much more sense than the one that he was making now.

Eddie looked at his watch. Pearl would be watching *Neighbours* now. He could see her resting on the sofa with a mug of tea, her head slowly falling then jerking upright as she struggled to stay awake. Pearl, his precious Pearl. He had always loved her name. It was different, classy. As he drove along, he tried to list all the pearly associations he could think of: pearl diver, Pearl Diver (the race horse), Pearl Bailey, pearl-barley, pearl buttons, 'String of Pearls' (the tune), string of pearls (round her neck), mother of pearl,

Pearl Harbor, pearly kings and queens, casting pearls before swine (him!) YES! definitely HIM! He was STUPID! STUPID! STUPID! risking his marriage for a stupid car!

He looked at his watch again and worked it out. Yes, he might just make it home if he put his foot down. He imagined her walking down the street exhausted after finishing work at the White Hart. Then, as she approached the house, she would notice the car on the drive and walk quicker, then start to run. (Eddie could hear her high heels clicking on the pavement.) 'Eddie! Eddie!' she would shout, as she burst into the living room and embraced him . . .

That was the U-certificate, family version. He revised the scene with a more plausible ending . . . Pearl notices the car on the drive and quickens her pace, then, bursting into the living room, yells, 'I thought I told you to get rid of that car!'

The ensuing mayhem would classify it X.

But it was his own stupid fault. He knew what her reaction would be when he bought the car, and who could blame her? He was too selfish. He was going to have to change his ways, there was no doubt about it. Resolution number 1 – sell the car; number 2 – smarten up and lose some weight. I'm turning into a big, fat slob. There's no wonder she's not interested in sex any more. Who wants a fucking hippo rolling on top of them in bed? If I'm not careful, she's going to leave me. And not over the car, either. She's not too old to get another feller. She's still a knock-out when she's dressed up. I've seen them looking at her. Dirty fuckers. She could still pull men if she wanted. And not old buggers like me, either. Young men. Young men fancy older women. It's a well-known fact. If Pearl had been driving the car back at the filling station, and the young bird inside had been a boy, he would have gone off with her if she had asked him. *She* didn't go off with me though, did she? And who can blame her? Who wants to ride with a Desperate Dan look-alike?

With his thoughts elsewhere, Eddie had been content to cruise along. But now, concentrating on the road again, he wanted to go faster, but every time he tried to overtake, the driver in front baulked him.

'Get over, you selfish bastard!' Eddie shouted, waving his arm.

The road was narrow and winding, with steep wooded banks, and it was too risky to overtake unless the driver in front pulled over and waved him past. A convoy had built up behind him and they too were sharing Eddie's frustration.

He's doing it out of spite. Jealously, that's what it is. He hates me because I'm driving something special and he's driving a boring old Nova. Eddie was tempted to ram him but he didn't want to damage the chrome bumper. As angry as he was, he still managed a smile at the thought of the driver's forehead smashing against the windscreen when he was hit from behind.

Calm down. Calm down, he ordered himself. You'll have a fucking heart attack if you're not careful. It was like a long fuse and when the driver in front picked up his mobile, the bomb exploded prematurely. It seemed like deliberate provocation to Eddie and, like Popeye, he had stood all he could stand and couldn't stand no more. Spinach coursed through his veins as he squeezed down on the accelerator and rumbled up alongside his tormentor, making no attempt to overtake. He was risking death and a multiple pile-up if another vehicle appeared round a bend. But he didn't care. He was past reason and intent on vengeance.

'You fucking road hog!'

There was madness in his eyes. Veering wildly, he leaned across and swung a right hook which just fell short, then reached out over the door and tried to turn the steering-wheel. The driver in the car directly behind Eddie leaned out of the window and egged him on.

'Go on, kill him! Kill the bastard!' he yelled, as Eddie reached across and tried to drag the road hog from his car. But Eddie was frustrated by the closing window and he thumped the glass in frustration.

'That'll not save you! You're a fucking dead man!'

Moments later, they nearly both were, as an ice-cream van appeared round a sharp bend. The traumatized driver instinctively swung the steering-wheel and his car left the road, leaving space for Eddie to move inside as the ice-cream van sped by safely. Eddie glanced through his rear-view mirror just before he disappeared round the bend. The Nova had settled amongst the brambles part way up the steep bank.

Eddie relaxed and started to laugh. Serves the bastard right. He'll have plenty to talk about on his mobile now. He was tempted to turn back and give the driver a right-hander while he was still fastened in his seat, but decided against it in case the police arrived and commenced their inquiries.

He started to laugh. Perhaps the ice-cream man had stopped and given the stunned driver a raspberry ripple to revive him. He laughed even louder at the thought of him fighting his way through the brambles with a dripping cornet, and the strapped-in driver phoning his wife to tell her that he would be late home for his tea. He hadn't laughed so much since Jason Reynolds had walked into the Greyhound wearing fifteen damp jumpers which he'd stolen from the launderette.

'Just one cornetto!' he sang, as he continued his journey. He decided against turning back. One night away wasn't dramatically going to alter the situation at home, and he knew that if he didn't complete his mission now, he would always regret it. He looked up as thunder rolled around the hills and dark clouds crossed the sun, draining colour from the land. It was time to find somewhere to stay before the storm broke.

He drove through lonely countryside, past isolated cottages and farms, and was beginning to wonder if he was going to have to spend the night in the car, when he finally reached a village and noticed a pub with a Vacancies sign in the window. He pulled up outside the front door and went inside. It was like entering a heritage pub, cleverly refurbished to represent bygone days. With its flagged floor and tobacco-stained walls, it reminded Eddie of the old city pubs where he used to drink with Jet before going on to the Cats Eyes. They would flounce in, resplendent in their Teddy-boy suits, and the regulars would laugh and shake their heads and wonder what the world was coming to.

The only other occupants of the bar were two old men playing cards, who looked as permanent as the fittings. They studied their hands for ages before laying down a card. Perhaps they had been playing since the fifties and had forgotten to go home, and their wives were still waiting for them with their dinners in the oven.

'Is there anybody about?'

Without looking up from his hand, one of the card players shouted, 'Fergus!'

Eddie waited for so long that he presumed Fergus was out or hadn't heard, but eventually the plastic curtain behind the bar parted and a man appeared, wiping his mouth on a bar towel. He was surprised to see Eddie. He had presumed that one of his regulars was calling for another drink, and decided that this was no reason to interrupt his dinner.

'Good evening. What can I get you?'

'Have you got a room for the night?'

The landlord folded the bar towel and hung it on the rail.

'I have.'

His admission was so grudging that Eddie wondered why he had bothered to advertise in the first place.

'How much?'

'Twenty pounds. Bed and breakfast.'

'How about food?'

'We do bar meals.'

'That'll do.'

'Would you like to see the room first?'

Eddie's immediate reaction was: why, what's wrong with it? Unless there was something spectacular to see, like a body in the wardrobe, he couldn't see the point.

The landlord pointed to a side door, which led into the hall.

'Up the stairs. Room number three. The door's unlocked.'

Eddie left the bar and glanced into the large, deserted lounge, with an unlit juke box in the corner, before going upstairs. A one-eyed stag's head mounted on a plaque and a grouse in a glass case decorated the walls on the landing. Although Eddie was no ornithologist, the egg between the grouse's feathered legs looked suspiciously like a hen's egg to him. He opened the door of his room and went in.

It was much as he expected: an old bed, cheap chest of drawers and wardrobe, and a wash basin in the corner. Except for the wash basin, it was similar to his bedroom at home when he was a boy. He sat on the bed to test the mattress. Years of heavy lifting in the steel works had left him with a bad back, and if he slept on a sagging mattress he had great difficulty putting on his socks next morning. But the mattress was firm, the pillows weighty, and laundry tickets were still stapled to the corners of the sheets like guarantees.

Eddie stood up and opened the window to let in fresh air. Although this room was similar to his childhood room, the view was entirely different. His window at home looked out across grey roofs and smoking chimneys, while this one framed a view of high hills and grazing sheep, with not a house in sight. Eddie breathed in the clean air, then lit a cigarette and, inspired by the solitude, he vowed to move to the country, grow vegetables and become a better man. On the strength of his resolution, he stubbed out his cigarette in the wash basin and left the room.

The card players were sweating over a twenty-pence kitty when Eddie returned to the bar. He picked up a menu from the counter then lit another cigarette and studied the dishes. He could have learned it off by heart by the time the landlord appeared through the curtain, accompanied by the closing theme music of *Coronation Street*. He pointed towards the window.

'There'll be some covetous eyes when they see yon motor, I can tell you!'

Eddie guessed that he was talking about his car, but the

accent plus the word before 'eyes', left him in some difficulty. Polish Jack who worked on the bins at home spoke clearer English than this bloke. He ordered the Pie of the Day with chips. He had expected to see something Scottish on the menu like haggis or cock-a-leekie soup, but it was no different to the menu at the Greyhound, except that here they didn't serve Yorkshire pudding with gravy. He ordered a pint of bitter while the landlord was present, in case he disappeared through the curtain and he never saw him again. Eddie hoped that they weren't screening an epic like *Ben Hur* on ITV. Adding on time taken by the news and commercial breaks, he could be facing starvation by the time it arrived. He thought of Pearl. She would have watched *Coronation Street* from behind the bar at the White Hart.

When it finally arrived, his meal was delicious. The vegetables were crisp and the chips, dipped in the thick gravy, tasted like the ones his mother used to fry in the chip pan, rather than the frozen, oven-baked variety he ate now.

He pushed away his empty plate, lit a cigarette and wondered how he was going to spend the rest of the evening. He didn't want to sit drinking on his own until closing time, so he decided to go up to his room for a rest, then come down later when there would probably be more customers in the bar and perhaps somebody to talk to.

On his way out, he asked the gamblers what time the pub closed.

'It depends,' one of them replied without looking up from his cards.

Eddie sang 'Stagger Lee' as he walked up the stairs. '*Two men they were gambling / Gambling in the dark.*' The one-eyed stag appeared to give Eddie a slow wink of approval when he reached the landing. Eddie winked back, then entered his room and lay down on the bed in the fading light. The silence was unnerving, as if the world had pitched camp and moved on. He sat up and looked out of the window to see if the hills were still there. Reassured by their massive bulk, he lay back on the unfamiliar, narrow mattress. It was the first time he had ever slept in a single bed since he'd got married. He felt the edges of the bedstead with his hands and feet, then turned on his side to see if there was any danger of rolling out while he was asleep. It was difficult to imagine that he had ever been small enough to burrow around in a bed this size and even more difficult to imagine that Carol had managed to squeeze in too, when she crept into his room to comfort him after Jack had given him a good hiding.

That bedroom of terror: waking to the sound of raised voices downstairs when Jack came in from the pub. His mother's sobs. The footsteps on the stairs. Then waiting, stiff with terror with his hands together imploring, No, God. Please, God. No. But worse than that, worse than all the beatings, was listening to Jack reading bedtime stores to Brenda and Carol in the next room. Listening to them laughing as he played the characters in different voices. He would get out of bed and stand on the cold lino with his ear pressed to the wall, straining to follow the story. Occasionally he would hear a wicked witch cackling, or the giant roaring, 'FE-FI-FO-FUM!' and he knew what was happening, because his mother read the same stories to him when Jack was out. But it was no consolation. He wanted to be included with his sisters in their big cosy bed.

*

169

Eddie opened his eyes. It was dark. He had no idea where he was. Elvis was singing 'Crying In The Chapel' somewhere nearby. He thought he had died and gone to rock 'n' roll heaven. Then he remembered and sat up on the bed. His meeting with the King would have to be postponed.

He switched on the bedside lamp, then stood up and crossed the room to the wash basin. Cool air ruffled the curtains at the open window and lightning briefly lit up the hills. He turned on the tap and started to count. He had reached ten and was drying his face by the time he heard the roll of thunder.

But he was more interested in what was happening down-stairs than in the impending storm. He could hear voices and laughter and 'Crying In The Chapel' had been replaced by 'Are Your Lonesome Tonight?' He had been so far; but judging by the sound of it, perhaps things were picking up.

He couldn't believe it when he left his room and went down. The place was crowded with people dressed in 1950s-style clothes. There were men wearing drape jackets and beetle-crusher shoes, and women with pencil skirts and pony-tails. Eddie couldn't understand it. Where had they all come from? Perhaps he *had* entered rock 'n' roll heaven after all. He had fallen asleep and woken up in 1956. Stagger Lee and Billy had finally departed from the bar and their seats had been taken by two old rockers dressed in Teddy-boy suits and bootlace ties.

In the lounge bar, an Elvis look-alike with a greased quiff was working a sound system in the corner of the room. *'Don't be cruel'*, he mimed, hunching over his mike. Eddie joined the crush at the bar and ordered a pint of bitter from a barmaid wearing a polka dot blouse and cut-off slacks.

'Do you take new money?' he asked, as she placed the glass on the bar.

'What do you mean?'

'I just wondered, you know, the way everybody's dressed. I thought you might be still using pounds, shillings and pence.'

He handed her a five-pound note and tried to guess her age. Late thirties? Early forties? Yes, she was old enough to remember the switch to decimalization, but he tried it on all the same.

'You're not old enough to remember the old money. The bank notes were as big as bed sheets. I once dropped a tenner into a puddle and I'd to hang it out on the clothes line to dry.'

The barmaid laughed and gave him his change.

'Of course I remember it.'

'I wouldn't have thought you were old enough.'

'I'm not. I've seen some in the museum in Glasgow.'

Eddie laughed.

'I suppose I asked for that.'

'Don't worry yourself. It's the most original chat-up line I've had in ages.'

'Would you like a drink?'

'No, thanks. Later perhaps.'

Eddie picked up his beer and looked around the crowded room.

'Talking about museums. This place was dead when I arrived. I can't believe it.'

'I know. When me and Joan advertised on local radio,' – she nodded towards the other barmaid, a woman closer to Eddie's age, with her greying hair pulled back into a pony-tail

– 'we'd no idea how many would turn up. It's fantastic. How did you find out?'

Eddie paused with his glass at his lips.

'Find out about what?'

The barmaid laughed.

'This!' indicating the crowded room. 'What do you think?'

Eddie shrugged, had a drink.

'I don't know. I'm just passing through.'

The barmaid served an ancient Teddy-boy wearing a maroon drape jacket with a black rolled collar. He exchanged nods with Eddie. It was like a war veterans' reunion.

The barmaid turned back to Eddie.

'Is that your car outside, the Cadillac?'

'Yeah.'

'I see! I thought somebody had hired it for the occasion.'

'Why, what's happening? Is it a fifties theme night or something?'

'No. It's an anniversary. It's twenty years today since Elvis died.'

Eddie placed two fingers to his head and crooked his thumb. Even though he had paid tribute earlier in the day, he hadn't made the connection. The last thing he expected to find out here in the wilds was an Elvis fan club. He couldn't imagine the Scots being keen on Elvis and rock 'n' roll. Bagpipes and kilts didn't go with the image some-how.

Eddie turned round and watched three couples jiving in the small space between the tables and the DJ. He thought of Pearl and how brilliantly they danced together and wondered how they would perform now. Pearl would still be nifty on her pins; she hadn't put on a pound since they met. But himself? The picture that came to mind was Ginger Rogers dancing with Bluto.

'Fat bastard,' Eddie muttered as he pulled in his stomach. He ordered another drink and asked the barmaid if she would like one too.

'Thanks. I'll have a Bud.'

Eddie felt himself blushing as she returned his gaze, and wondered if his heartbeat showed through his commemorative T-shirt.

'OK you guys! This is the moment you've been waiting for! It's karaoke time!'

Whistles and applause greeted the DJ's announcement. The barmaid winked at Eddie and went back to work.

'We'll start at the beginning. Where else? It's 1956 and "Hound Dog"!'

Eddie had first heard it on Radio Luxembourg after reading about Elvis in *Record Mirror*, which Jack used to make the fire with if he found it lying around the house.

'Call that bloody music?' he used to shout, screwing up the pages and stuffing them into the grate. 'They ought to behead the buggers like the Japs used to do in Burma!' And Eddie used to imagine his idols like Elvis and Chuck Berry on their knees with their necks on a chopping block. He would stand behind him with his fists clenched and plan retaliatory executions for Jack's favourite singers: Vera Lynn, Donald Peers and Doris Day; boring old squares who looked as old as his parents. Then he would run upstairs and, safe in his bedroom, defiantly turn up his collar and play air guitar in front of the wardrobe mirror.

Eddie smiled to himself as he remembered how Jet and he used to call each other 'E' and 'hillbilly cat', and try to speak with a Yankee drawl when they went out together.

'Fancy a pint, E?' Jet would ask him.

'Sure would, you hillbilly cat,' Eddie would reply. 'I've worked up one hell of a thirst after recording all day.'

'So what's the new disc called, E?'

'"Heartbreak Hotel". It sure is a winner, I can tell you.'

Then they would face each other at the bar and sob the lyrics into imaginary hand mikes.

Eddie returned to the Scottish bar with tears in his eyes. A man wearing a check shirt and jeans was singing 'Good Luck Charm'. The words, lit up on the screen behind him, were superfluous because the audience knew all the songs off by heart.

But Eddie didn't join in. He was growing increasingly maudlin as he thought about Jet and the crazy times they had enjoyed together. If he had been here now, they would have performed their Elvis double act. They might even have gone on and become world famous, like the Everly Brothers.

Eddie felt someone touch his arm. He turned round, expecting to see Jet, but saw the barmaid instead.

'Are you all right?'

Eddie stared at her, re-focusing.

'You were miles away.'

He nodded, slowly.

'Yeah.'

'You looked sad.'

'It's the music. It takes you back.'

The vocalist in the check shirt finished his number and Eddie eased his way between the tables and took the mike. He turned to the DJ.

' "Heartbreak Hotel".' He wrapped the lead round his hand and set himself with his left foot forward. 'This one's for you, kid, wherever you are.'

His sentimental dedication caused a hush in the room. They thought it was meant for Elvis, but they were wrong.

Well since my baby left me
Well I've found a new place to dwell . . .

Eddie closed his eyes and jerked his leg in time to the music. His voice wasn't as good as the previous singer's, but he made up for it by the sheer intensity of his delivery. Hunched over the mike, shoulders twitching, he wasn't just singing the song, he was living it.

Well I'll be,
I'll be just so lonely, baby.

Jet, Elvis, his father and mother, all gone. And now Pearl . . .

Down at the end of lonely street
That Heartbreak Hotel.

Nobody sang along with him. It wasn't party time. They had never seen a lonelier man in their lives. A man so lonely, he could die.

As the final guitar chords faded, Eddie stood with his head bowed, eyes closed. He was breathing hard and sweating. There was no applause or movement in the audience. They had just seen a man grieving publicly and they weren't sure how to respond. A flash of lightning lit the stained-glass windows and, as the thunder rolled, Eddie opened his eyes and left the room. He stood in the hall doorway watching the storm while he composed himself, then he stepped outside and turned his face up to the cooling rain.

'What are you doing?'

Eddie turned round. The barmaid was standing in the doorway, trying to avoid the rain. She grabbed Eddie's arm and pulled him inside.

'You'll catch your death of cold out there.'

Eddie smoothed back his hair and wiped his hands on his jeans.

'I was just cooling off.'

'I thought you'd left.'

'I'd be a fool to travel in this weather, wouldn't I?'

'You certainly would.'

They smiled at each other. Eddie lifted up the sleeve of his T-shirt and wiped his face.

'I'd better go upstairs and dry off.'

'OK. By the way, what's your name?'

Eddie looked puzzled.

'I thought I told you.'

'No. It just seems that way.'

'What do you mean?'

'As if we know each other.'

Eddie held her gaze and smiled.

'I'm Eddie. Pleased to meet you, Sue.'

She looked startled.

'How do you know my name?'

'I heard one of the customers call you it.' He moved towards the stairs. 'I'll be down in a few minutes.'

'Perhaps you could give us an encore?'

They listened to the applause at the end of 'Wooden Heart'. Eddie shook his head.

'It won't be that one. That is for sure.'

'Why not?'

'It's the only Elvis song I don't like. It always reminds me of *Pinocchio*.'

Eddie went upstairs and pressed the light button on the landing but it went dark again almost immediately.

'Tight bastard,' Eddie grumbled as he fumbled his key into the lock.

Rain had blown in through the open window and formed a pool on the window ledge. Eddie closed the window, then mopped up the water with the bottom of the curtains and wrung them out in the sink. He started to take off his damp T-shirt, then remembered that he had left his old one in the car. He paused, chest exposed before the mirror, debating whether to fetch it or not . . . By the time he had run out to the car, unlocked the door and run back again, he would be soaked. He decided to keep his damp one on. It would soon dry out in the lounge. Anyway, it was fitting that he should wear it for the commemorative karaoke, even if it was uncomfortable. It was proof of his loyalty. A hair-shirt gesture of devotion to his idol.

As he combed his hair in front of the mirror, he thought about Sue. Not in an overtly sexual way like he thought about the girls in skimpy frocks who met in the Greyhound for a quick drink before going clubbing in town. Especially that big, blonde girl, Maxine! No. No. It wasn't like that. Although she *was* attractive. And she had a nice smile. And he could tell from the start that she liked him. And that was *before* he sang 'Heartbreak Hotel'.

Eddie tucked in his T-shirt and prepared to go downstairs. He anticipated a standing ovation when he entered the lounge.

Then, after persistent demands for an encore, he would give in and have them jiving on the tables with 'Jailhouse Rock'.

But when he reached the bottom of the stairs, he was disappointed to see that people were leaving. He couldn't understand it. The karaoke wasn't over because he could hear somebody singing. He must be bad, Eddie thought, if he's driving them out into a thunder storm.

When he entered the lounge he saw the reason: two skinheads were standing by the karaoke machine, bent on trouble. Eddie walked across to the bar. Sue smiled a him. She looked pleased to see him. Eddie ordered a pint and nodded towards the skinheads.

'Who are they?'

'Them? Two of Scotland's finest. Just ignore them.'

But it was easier said than done. They were jeering the vocalist, banging into the tables and trying to provoke fights by accusing people of staring at them. But worst of all, in Eddie's eyes, they were insulting the music and the occasion. A tribute to the finest singer who had ever lived was being ruined by a couple of barbarians. Eddie sized them up. They were big lads, wearing regulation dockers, tight jeans and bomber jackets, but he decided they were too noisy to be dangerous. In his experience, it was the silent types you had to watch out for.

An old Scottish Ted, wearing a plaid Teddy-boy suit, defiantly took the mike and asked the DJ to play 'Love Me Tender'. Eddie could never hear this song without becoming sentimental and thinking of Pearl, even now, when it was being sung in an unfamiliar Scottish accent. *For you make my life complete/And I love you so.* Eddie turned away from the bar so that Sue couldn't see his tears. Then the skinheads started whistling. Piercing, two-fingers in the mouth whistling, as if they were whistling a dog. Eddie stepped forward and jabbed a finger at them.

'You two! Shut it!'

The skinheads turned and stared at him with their fingers still stuck in their mouths. Then they squared up to him displaying tattooed knuckles.

'Are you talking to us, mister?'

Eddie was in no mood for B-movie dialogue.

'No. I'm talking to that fucking rabbit up there.'

He pointed to a stuffed rabbit mounted in a glass case above the mirror behind the bar. If he had opted for the adjoining wild cat, the skinheads wouldn't have felt so insulted.

The old cunt was looking for trouble, no doubt about it. But he was a mean-looking bastard, all the same.

'So what you going to do about it then, Grandad?'

'I'll tell you what I'm going to do . . .' Eddie took another step forward. 'If you don't show a bit of respect, I'll batter you. And when I've battered you, I'll throw you out and batter you again.'

Somebody laughed. The skinheads glared around the room. They were under pressure. They had to respond to Eddie's threat or back down and lose face. The tall one, with a line of rings decorating his ear, walked up to Eddie and thrust his face at him.

'Do you think we're scared of you, you fat bastard?'

Poor lad. If he had pondered all day, he couldn't have chosen a more lethal combination. Fat, on its own, would have earned him a black eye, but linked to bastard, he was in serious trouble. Eddie grabbed his lapels and nutted him. There was a snap of breaking bone and Eddie pushed him away as the blood gushed from his nose. The youth staggered backwards, holding his face.

'My nose! You've broken my fucking nose!'

'Don't worry. This'll take your mind off it.'

Eddie kicked him in the balls and sent him crashing amongst the tables. His mate was looking around wildly for a way out, but Eddie was positioned between him and the door. He backed away as Eddie moved towards him, then produced a flick knife from his back pocket and clicked out the blade.

'Come on, then. Come on.'

He beckoned Eddie towards him as though guiding him into a parking space. Eddie picked up a bar stood and knocked him to the floor. He kicked away the knife, then, as he yanked him to his feet to hit him again, he noticed the swastika tattooed on the back of the youth's hand. Eddie held him by the wrist and stared at it.

'Bastard! Where'd you get this done, in prison?'

'What's it to you?'

Eddie slapped him across the face.

'I did it myself.'

'Yeah, and I'll tell you why. Because you couldn't find a tattooist to do it, could you?'

The skinhead remained silent. The eagle on Eddie's fore-arm looked poised to take off for his throat.

'You fucking retard! Have you any idea what the Nazis were like? What'd have happened if they'd come over here?'

Eddie shook his wrist so hard, that his skull-and-crossbones ring worked loose and fell to the floor. Eddie waited for it to stop bouncing then stamped on it.

'Millions of people died because of them bastards. My

dad . . .' He paused, too choked to continue for a moment or two. 'My dad was a pilot on bombing missions over Germany. Every time he took off he never knew if he was going to come back alive. Hamburg, Berlin, under fire all the time from anti-aircraft guns and Messerschmitts. And then one time he didn't come back. He was reported missing and my mother . . . my mother never knew what happened to him up to the day she died.'

The youth, gripped by the shirt front and fearing further assault, found it difficult to concentrate on what Eddie was saying. He would have preferred the Nazis any day.

Eddie pushed him away, sending him crashing amongst the tables.

'Go on! Get out while you're still safe!'

Safe was the last thing the skinheads felt as they hobbled from the room under Eddie's malevolent eye. He expected departing threats and obscenities, and perhaps a brick through the window, but nothing happened and he had a drink to calm down while Sue and Joan and the remaining Elvis fans tidied up the room.

When all the tables and chairs were back in place and the broken glass had been swept up, the DJ tried to rescue the evening by resuming the karaoke. A man in lime-green socks responded with 'King Creole', but the violence had ruined the occasion, there were no more volunteers, and by closing time the DJ had departed and Eddie was the only customer left in the bar.

'Sorry about that,' Eddie said, watching Sue trying to mend the broken stool.

'Don't worry about it. They deserved everything they got.'

'Let me have a go. I was top in woodwork at school.'

Sue shook her head.

'There's no point. The legs are all cracked.'

Joan left the room and returned moments later with the news that the rain had stopped and she was going home.

'O K, Joan. I'll see you tomorrow.'

Eddie apologized again for spoiling the evening.

'Not to worry,' Joan said. 'I enjoyed it. We don't get much excitement round here.'

She left the room and Eddie and Sue listened to the door closing as she went out.

'I'd better go to bed,' Eddie said, picking up the pieces of a broken ashtray. 'Then you can go home.'

'That's O K. I've got a bit of tidying up to do first. Would you like another drink?'

Eddie looked up at the clock on the wall above the stuffed rabbit.

'Don't worry about the time. You're a resident. You can drink as long as you like.'

Eddie wished that the same residential rules applied at home. Pearl objected bitterly to him settling down to a late night movie on television with a six pack, when she had to get up for work at half past five next morning.

'O K. I'll have a scotch. How about you?'

'Thanks. I'll have the same, if that's all right?'

She drained the measures from the optic. Eddie chased the melting ice cubes round the bucket and spooned a couple into his glass. Sue took hers neat. They raised their glasses.

'Cheers.'

Eddie lit a cigarette, then walked across to the mini juke box attached to the wall at the end of the bar and flicked through the play lists . . . Golden Oldies, Easy Listening, Rock 'n' Roll.

'I hate these little juke boxes. It's more like making a phone call than choosing a record.'

He made his selections, then returned to Sue, who was washing out the drip trays.

'You seem to run this place.'

Sue nodded. 'I suppose I do really. I started working here when the bakery in the village closed down and it developed from there. Fergus isn't the most dynamic landlord in the business, as you've probably noticed. He just lets me get on with it.'

'So I've noticed. I was surprised he didn't show up during the ruckus.'

'He'd have been in the back watching the telly. Or in bed. On my nights off, the regulars serve themselves and chalk it up on the slate.' They laughed. Sue hung up the bar towels. 'I only live across the road. It's dead handy. I enjoy it. You know, the company and that.'

Eddie nodded. He knew all right. Sometimes, when Pearl wasn't talking to him, he thought of asking the landlord of the Greyhound if he had a room to let. The pub opened at 10.00 a.m. They served food all day. He could play darts, pool, dominoes and cards. He could play the juke box and watch the telly in the tap room. There were quiz nights, karaokes and bands, and, best of all, hen parties, with the prospect of a quick one upstairs with a glamorous granny. He could lead a full and active life, seven days a week, without stepping out of the door. Sheer paradise. Or at least the closest Eddie was likely to get to it.

'I like your car. Are you up here on holiday?'

Eddie ducked the ice cubes in his glass while he considered the question.

'Sort of. You know, touring around.'

'You don't seem to be having a very good time.'

Eddie looked at her, surprised.

'I'm having a great time. Why do you say that?'

'You seem troubled. You know, "Heartbreak Hotel", then the fight . . .'

'They deserved everything they got! Nazi scumbags!'

'I agree. But it seemed personal. You know, deeper somehow.'

'Dead right. It *was* personal. It was my dad!'

Sue reached across the bar and squeezed his hand.

'I'm sorry. I didn't mean anything.'

Eddie took out his handkerchief and blew his nose.

'It's funny, isn't it? You think you're grown up, then something happens that knocks you off your feet and you want to run home to your mother.'

'I think everybody feels like that sometimes.'

Eddie wiped his eyes and blew his nose again.

'Take no notice of me. It's the drink talking. I think I'd better go to bed. It's been a long day.'

'Would you like a coffee before you go up?'

Eddie paused then nodded.

'That'd be nice. As long as I'm not keeping you up.'

He expected her to produce two mugs and a jar of coffee from behind the bar, but instead, she lifted up the counter and came out into the room.

'I'll just put out the lights.'

Eddie stared at her, puzzled.

'What for?'

He couldn't see the point of drinking coffee in the dark.

'Because I'm going home. Why do you think?'

The storm had passed and the night was misty and still. Eddie walked round his car, checking that the skinheads hadn't scarred the paintwork with a blade in revenge, then he stood on the pavement, enjoying the silence and the cool air on his face.

'It's never like this in town. Even when it's quiet in the middle of the night you can always hear something. Especially where I live.'

'Yes. It's a bit too quiet sometimes. Like a graveyard.'

The click of Sue's heels was so loud as they crossed the road that Eddie was convinced they must be under surveillance from behind the curtains of every house in the row. She unlocked the front door of the end house and Eddie followed her inside.

'Hang on a minute while I switch the light on.'

She crossed the room in the darkness, and when she switched on the standard lamp in the corner, its dull light was enriched by the glowing colours of a Wurlitzer juke box standing massively against the wall, which lit up simul-taneously.

'Christ!'

Eddie stood in the doorway, mesmerized.

Sue laughed.

'You didn't expect that, did you?'

Eddie walked across the room and stood in front of the juke box, staring down through the glass dome at the stack of records beside the turntable and card-list of Elvis titles. A faded label on the glass read: I play 10c, 3 plays 25c.

Eddie just stood there, shaking his head.

'It's fantastic.'

'I thought you'd like it.'

'I mean . . .' He paused, struggling to translate his feelings into words.

'It's like a personal shrine. Having an altar in your own house.'

'Play something if you like. Keep the volume down though. I don't want to wake the neighbours.'

Eddie thought of his own noisy neighbour, then imagined a kilted Jock battering the wall down with a caber.

'I haven't got ten cents.'

She laughed.

'Just make your selection and press the start button. It's been adapted. It's free.'

Free plays on a Wurtlizer stacked with Elvis records! He had crossed the road and entered paradise.

'I'll go and put the kettle on.'

She went into the kitchen and switched on the light. As Eddie selected his records, he remembered standing by the juke box in the Cats Eyes and selecting records with Jet.

'Where did you get it from?'

'The pub. Fergus decided it was time to enter the twentieth century. He was talking about turning the lounge into a disco with flashing lights and all that. I mean, can you imagine, out here in the wilds? He got as far as changing the juke box and that was about it. He lost interest. I don't think he liked the idea of attracting customers in the end. It might have been too much like hard work. Anyway, it turned out all right for me because he sold me the old juke box cheap.'

Eddie was so thrilled with the juke box that he had barely

noticed the rest of the room. He watched the stylus settle on 'Good Luck Charm', then looked around.

The walls were decorated with Elvis photographs, and a life-size tapestry of Elvis in a white spangled suit hung from the picture rail in an alcove by the fireplace. Eddie crossed the room and stood before it. Blurring the figure through narrowed eyes and listening to the record, Eddie imagined that he was standing at the front of the stage at an Elvis concert.

Sue came through from the kitchen, carrying a tray containing two mugs decorated with Elvis portraits, and an Elvis milk jug, with his quiff forming the spout.

'Do you like it?'

Eddie turned round from the tapestry.

'Yeah, it's great.'

'It was a present from Hong Kong.'

She placed the tray on the coffee table and sat down on the sofa. Eddie sat down beside her. When they picked up their mugs, they revealed a picture of Elvis sitting at the wheel of a Cadillac.

'That's a present from Spain.'

Eddie laughed.

'He sure gets around.'

Sue started to get up.

'I'm sorry. Do you take sugar?'

'No, thanks.'

Eddie had given up sugar to try to lose weight, but he was tempted to renege just to see what the sugar basin looked like.

'It's the beer you need to cut out,' Pearl had replied when he announced his intention to diet. That was five years ago. He was still working on it.

A podgy-looking Elvis decked out in a gold lamé suit sneered down at him from the wall. Eddie sneered back. Talk about the frying pan calling the kettle black! He looked around the room.

'It's like a shrine in here. You could charge an entrance fee.'

'It's silly really, I suppose. Somebody my age.'

'You don't look old enough to be an Elvis fan.'

She nudged him and laughed.

'I like it! Keep going!'

'I mean an original fan from the fifties, like me. I'd have thought the sixties was more your era. You know, the Beatles and Rolling Stones and all that.'

'It was. But my older brother was an Elvis freak. He had all his records and I followed on from him. I liked the Beatles, and Bob Dylan, and some of the others, but they couldn't hold a candle to Elvis.'

Eddie sat back and stared across the room at a photograph of Elvis in his army uniform.

'Yeah, it was a great time, the fifties and rock 'n' roll. It's been downhill all the way since then.'

Sue pointed at the bonnet of Elvis's Cadillac protruding from under her mug.

'That's like your car.'

'Yeah, similar. It's a bit later though. It's a 57 Biarritz convertible. Mine's a 55 Eldorado.'

'Have you had it long?'

Eddie sipped his coffee.

'About two years. It's been a life-long ambition to own a Cadillac. I worked every hour that God sent and saved up for it.'

Sue stood up and walked across to the juke box.

'What would you like on?'

'Anything. You choose.'

While she was selecting the records, Eddie lifted her mug off the Cadillac and allowed Elvis to breathe again. Sue waited for the introduction, before sitting down again next to Eddie.

'Would you like another coffee?'

'No, thanks.'

'Beer?'

Eddie hesitated then shook his head.

'I'd better not. I've got a long day tomorrow.'

'Where are you going?'

'Oh, you know . . . "Riding along in my automobile".'

Sue immediately picked up on the Chuck Berry reference,

'"Baby beside me at the wheel".'

Eddie stared morosely at the goldfish circling the bowl on top of the television set.

'Do you think goldfish get lonely?'

Sue stared at him and laughed.

'I don't know. It's hard to tell with goldfish. They've got pretty restricted body language.'

'Their fins go down sometimes.'

'That's when they're ill.'

'Perhaps they get ill when they're lonely.'

'Who knows?'

Eddie watched the goldfish swimming on the spot, gulping at the glass wall.

'Do you remember that goldfish on the Tweetie Pie cartoons that used to flutter its eyelashes and smack its lips at the cat?'

'Vaguely.'

'I always wanted a goldfish like that. You know, one with a proper face that looked pleased when it saw you.'

'They're hard to come by.'

Sue placed her hand on Eddie's arm.

'Are you married?'

Eddie paused, still watching the goldfish.

'Yeah, just about.'

'Any children?'

'A boy and a girl. They're grown up now. Got kids of their own. What about you?'

'I'm divorced. I've got a son. He's working in Australia. The last time I heard from him he was on the Barrier Reef.'

'Plenty of goldfish there.'

Sue laughed. Eddie stared at the blank screen of the television set.

'I once won a goldfish at the fair. My mother bought me a goldfish bowl and I put some pebbles in and fetched some weed from the pond. It looked really nice. I was proud of it. It was the first pet I ever had. Then, one night, my stepfather came home from the pub blind drunk and after a row with my mother, he tipped it down the toilet. I was heartbroken.'

'I can imagine.'

'I can understand it now, though. He'd had a rough time during the war and when he came back things didn't turn out for him.'

'I know the feeling.'

'Yeah. Same here.'

'You're just a big softie really, aren't you? All that hard-man stuff and tattoos.'

Sue traced her forefinger up the body of a snake coiled around a dagger on his bicep. When she lifted up the sleeve of his T-shirt to reach its head, she uncovered his latest addition.

'Is this a new one?'

'Yeah. I had it done this morning.'

She ran her fingers gently across the row of numbers.

'It looks sore.'

Eddie looked down at her painted nails and wedding ring on her right hand.

'It's OK.'

'I'll bathe it for you.'

'Don't put yourself about. It'll be better in the morning.'

Sue stood up and went through into the kitchen. Eddie sang along quietly to 'Teddy Bear', until she returned carrying a steaming basin and a clean tea towel. She placed the basin on the coffee table, then sat down again and unfolded the towel, revealing a portrait of Elvis printed on the material. When she held it up to show Eddie, the creases in the material made Elvis look as if he was smiling at them through a window.

'I've put a drop of Dettol in the water to soothe it.'

She dipped a corner of the towel into the water and dabbed the inflamed flesh around the tattoo. Then, holding up the towel in front of Eddie, she shouted.

'Private Presley, 53310761. Reporting for duty, sir.'

Eddie stared at her, amazed.

'How did you know that?'

'I told you. I'm an Elvis fan.'

'Yeah, I know, but that's *University Challenge* stuff.'

'Ask me any question you like.'

Eddie sat back and closed his eyes, as Sue played nurse again.

'That feels good.'

'That's not a question.'

'OK. What date was Elvis enlisted?'

'March twenty-fourth 1958.'

'What time?'

'Six-thirty a.m.'

Eddie paused. It seemed a bit early in the day to him. But as he didn't know himself, and she answered with such conviction, he let it pass.

'What date did he get married?'

'May first 1967. At the Aladdin Hotel, Las Vegas.'

Eddie was impressed. He knew the date and location but he didn't know the venue.

'It's my turn now.'

Sue patted Eddie's arm dry.

'Can you remember where you were when you heard that Elvis was dead?'

Eddie sat up and stared at the goldfish.

'Yeah. I was at work.' He turned to Sue. 'What about you?'

'We were on holiday in a caravan at Whitley Bay. I heard it on the radio. I went outside. I was in total shock. It was hot and there was a plague of ladybirds that year and my son Stewart, he was only a wean then, had picked one up and he was trying to peel the shell off it, I was horrified. I said, "What are you doing?" He said, "I'm taking it's jacket off because it's too hot!"'

They laughed. Sue wiped her eyes on the tea towel then touched Eddie's new tattoo.

'Is that why you had this done, to commemorate Elvis's death?'

Eddie looked away.

'Sort of.'

Sue moved close and slid her arm around his shoulders.

'Eddie. I don't know what's gone wrong, or what you're doing here. It's none of my business. But one thing I do know, that under all that hard-man stuff I think you're a really nice guy.'

'Thanks.'

If it hadn't been for the 'hard-man stuff' he would have taken the tea towel and dabbed his eyes. Instead, he put his arms around her and kissed her. She was smaller and slimmer than Pearl, and felt more like a girl in his arms. It was a novelty, necking on the sofa, he hadn't done it for years. At home, they always did it in bed. A quick fumble, followed by a quick fuck, then falling asleep with their backs to each other. Pearl was always so tired. He felt that if he didn't get on with it, she would fall asleep underneath him. It was like working against an egg-timer. Three minutes and his time was up.

But it hadn't always been like that. When they were courting, and Pearl's mother and father went out for the evening, they would stack up the records on the radiogram, switch off the light, then neck on the sofa in front of the fire. After the prelude of French kissing, Eddie would slip his hand up her jumper and fondle her breasts, and sometimes his fingers would tremble so much with excitement that Pearl would have to reach behind her and unfasten the bra hooks herself.

*

'Come on. Let's go to bed.'

Sue switched off the light and Eddie felt like an intruder as he followed her up the unfamiliar, dog-legged stairs. He laughed when he reached the landing and saw the flushed doors fitted with plastic handles set at an angle on the hardboard.

'It's like a 1950s museum in here.'

'What do you mean?'

'The flushed doors. They were all the rage when I was a kid.'

She walked into her bedroom and switched on the bedside lamp.

'They were like that when I moved in. I was going to take the hardboard off, but I never got round to it.'

Except for his mother's, which didn't count, Eddie had never been in another woman's bedroom. He stood in the doorway embarrassed. Whenever he had fantasized about sex – usually when he was having it with Pearl – it always occurred on neutral territory, like the back seat of a car or an indeterminate room. The intimacy of Sue's bedroom, with its personal belongings, made him uneasy. He half expected to hear a key in the front door.

'Where's the bathroom?'

'Next door.'

Eddie stood at the lavatory staring down into the bowl but nothing happened. He tried to relax by reading the labels on the cosmetics on a shelf above the wash basin, but when he noticed the same brand of deodorant that Pearl used, he hurriedly flushed the lavatory and returned to the bedroom.

Sue was sitting on the bed wearing her knickers and bra. Eddie started to undress, leaving his jeans until last; but when he unzipped the fly and pulled them down, he was horrified to see that he was wearing the Mickey Mouse underpants that his grandson Jason had bought him for a Christmas present. He blushed and felt the sweat break out on his face. He didn't know whether to bluff it out and continue undressing with feigned indifference, or pull up his jeans and remove the two garments simultaneously, hoping that Sue hadn't noticed the offending pants.

But it was too late. She started to laugh, but affectionately, as if she was watching a Mickey Mouse cartoon. Eddie laughed too.

'I'd have worn my silk boxer shorts if I'd known this was going to happen. It was the last thing I expected when I set off.'

Eddie undressed then sat on the bed next to Sue.

'What were you expecting?'

'I wasn't expecting anything. I just wanted to get away.'

'And now you're here.'

'Yeah. I can't believe it.'

Sue undressed and they lay down on the bed together and kissed. Eddie had forgotten what it felt like to be wanted. 'Yes, Eddie. Yes . . .' A different voice. A different body with different moves and surprises. 'Yes. Yes . . .' She was astride him now, her breasts heavy as she leaned over him, then tightening as she arched back. Eddie pushed against her, thrusting his hips. 'Oh, my God. Yes. Yes. Yes!' Sue bowed her head, sobbing with emotion. Eddie pulled her to him and embraced her, and they lay in each other's arms for a long time before Sue kissed him gently on the cheek and switched off the bedside lamp.

Eddie lay in the dark, staring at the window. He couldn't

195

believe how quiet it was. No joy riders tearing past. No drunks. No fights. No late night cabs and slamming doors. No sirens and no music thudding through the wall from next door. Just silence. Pure, clear silence . . .

When Eddie woke up, it was light outside. At first, he thought he was at home. Then he didn't know where he was. Then he remembered. He raised his head and looked over his shoulder. Sue had her back towards him, revealing the vulnerable nape of her neck. He edged out of bed and dressed quietly, holding the buckle of his belt to stop it rattling when he pulled up his jeans. He decided to put on his shoes downstairs, but even crossing the floor in his stockinged feet, he couldn't stop the floorboards creaking. Strange how he hadn't heard them last night.

'Eddie.'

He paused at the door and turned round. Sue was smiling at him from the bed.

'I didn't want to wake you.'

He walked back to the bed and crouched down. Sue reached out and held his hand.

'I'm glad you did.'

Eddie hugged her through the covers and stroked back her hair from her face.

'It's been great, thanks.'

'Look after yourself, Eddie.'

'And you.'

'If you're up here again, you know where I am.'

'Yeah. Thanks.'

Eddie leaned over and kissed her lightly on the lips, as if he was kissing a child goodnight. Then he went downstairs and left the house, quietly closing the door behind him.

The early morning air was cool after the storm and thick mist obscured the hills behind the pub. There was no one about and no traffic on the road. It was so quiet that Eddie could hear a dog barking somewhere in the far distance. He walked across to his car. The roof was still damp from the downpour and the raindrops sparkled like spilled diamonds on the waxed bonnet.

Eddie unlocked the door, then sat at the wheel, staring across at Sue's house. He didn't want to leave her. They had got on so well together, it was as if they had known each other for years. He thought of her lying in bed. Would she have gone back to sleep? Or would she be awake, thinking about him and wishing that he hadn't gone? Then he remembered something and smiled to himself. He got out of the car, opened the boot and took out his rolled-up portrait. Unable to resist a last peep, he unrolled it and a young, handsome dude in a Hawaiian shirt smiled up at him. Eddie smiled back, marvelling at the artist's skill at achieving such a likeness. He rolled up the portrait and crossed the road again to Sue's house. Carefully, holding the flap open so that it wouldn't snap shut and disturb her, Eddie slid the tube through the letter box then, resisting the temptation to look up at her bedroom window, he returned to his car and drove away.

What would she make of his gesture? Would she be amused or sad? But whatever conclusion she reached, at least she would know that he had not regarded their brief time together as a mere one-night stand.

It was time for some music. He played a tape of Elvis ballads as he cruised through the quiet countryside with the slow drag of the windscreen wipers matching his mellow mood. '*Are you lonesome tonight? La-La-La-La-La-La,*' he sang softly as he pulled in at a roadside café. He bought a local newspaper, then ordered the All Day Breakfast and sat by the window where he could keep an eye on his car. On an inside page of the paper, he noticed a story about the driver of a hearse who had been arrested for speeding. He had told the police that due to unforeseen circumstances he was late for the funeral, and if they didn't arrive at the cemetery in time it would have to be postponed. The mourners in the following car were said to be terrified and hysterical as it tried to keep up with the hearse, which was reportedly travelling at 90 m.p.h.

Eddie was still grinning at the thought of it as he left the café and resumed his journey. He passed through a former mining village where the Workingmen's Club had been converted into a Heritage Centre and the muck stack contoured into a ski slope. Then, after passing the entrance to the Tam O' Shanter Experience, he saw the road sign ahead: Kilmarnock, Irvine and finally, Prestwick Airport. At last! They had finally made it after all those years. Eddie couldn't have been more excited if he had seen a sign post for Graceland or Memphis, Tennessee.

'We've done it, kid! We're nearly there!'

Eddie, still wearing his overalls from work, was having his tea when Jet rushed into the living room waving the *Evening Post*.

'Seen this? It's fantastic!'

Eddie knew that it must be something important, because he always knocked on the door to the tune of 'Woody Woodpecker' before entering.

'What? What is it?'

'This!'

With shaking hands, Jet pushed the newspaper in front of Eddie's face.

'Elvis! He's been demobbed from the army and he landed at Prestwick Airport on his way back to America from Germany!'

'Prestwick? Where's that?'

'I don't know. In Scotland somewhere. His plane landed there for refuelling.'

Eddie snatched the paper from him and scanned the report. ' "Standing on the runway surrounded by adoring fans, Elvis was asked if he would like to return someday. 'I sure would like to tour the British Isles,' he replied, flashing that famous grin . . ." '

'Lucky sods. Just imagine standing next to Elvis.'

'Yeah. And touching him. I'd wear a glove on that hand for ever.'

'Yeah. And talking to him.'

'Yeah. And getting his autograph.'

'Yeah. I wish we'd known.'

'Yeah. We could have gone.'

'Yeah. In a taxi.'

'Yeah. Prestwick Airport, Mac. And step on the gas!'

They laughed and Eddie stood up and fetched the atlas from the sideboard. He pushed away his unfinished meal to make room on the tablecloth, then turned to the map of the British Isles. Edinburgh and Glasgow were obvious in thick, black print, but during their search for Prestwick they discovered the location of towns they had known previously only from the football results. Jet shook his head.

'It's not on.'

'It must be. Let's start at Solway Firth and work up.'

They hummed 'All Shook Up' as their fingers criss-crossed the map, meandering north. Then Eddie ended the duet when he stabbed the page and shouted, 'There!'

And there it was, on the west coast just above Ayr: Prestwick, their new-found Mecca. Eddie kept his finger on the map, directing their gaze like a signpost.

'Just imagine being there when he stepped off the plane.'

'Yeah. It must have been fantastic.'

Their tone was reverential and Eddie imagined Elvis standing in the doorway of the aeroplane, with his arms raised and a halo round his army cap, blessing the kneeling disciples on the runway. Then, abruptly and without explanation, he turned the pages to the map of Europe.

'What are you doing?'

Jet sounded peeved. He wanted to prolong the romance of Prestwick.

'I've just thought of something.'

He picked up the bread knife and, using it as a ruler, positioned it diagonally across Europe.

'Look!'

Bemused, Jet obeyed him, but all he could see was a bread knife bridging the English Channel, and crumbs scattered across France. With mounting excitement, Eddie traced the route along the knife edge from Germany up to Scotland.

'Look where the flight path goes: through Belgium, then over into East Anglia, then up through the Midlands into Yorkshire. And look! It goes right over here!'

They stared at each other, digesting the significance of Eddie's navigational skills, then dashed outside and stood on the path gazing up at the clear, starlit sky.

'Just think.' Eddie paused. 'Elvis might have flown over our house.'

They fell silent, overcome by the enormity of such an occurrence. Eddie focused on a star which appeared to be blinking and continually changing colour and imagined it was Elvis's aeroplane. He used his fist for a microphone.

'Ground control to Elvis. Do you read me? Over.'

Jet stared at him. Eddie repeated the message.

'Do you read me, Elvis? Over.'

Jet laughed and spoke into his cupped hand.

'Ah sure do hear you, you hillbilly cat. This is Elvis, Elvis over England, reading you loud and clear.'

They were unable to continue their exchange for laughing, and a passing neighbour, observing the two boys hanging on to each other, thought they were drunk.

Eddie cleared his throat and composed himself.

'I wonder if you could tell us, Elvis, me and my mate Jet who's standing here with me, what your plans are now that you've finished your National Service? Over.'

Jet turned away so their eyes wouldn't meet.

'Well, I aim to resume my recording career and maybe make some more movies. That's as much as I can tell you right now. Over.'

'Have you any plans to come to England in the future? We'd love to meet you over here. Over.'

'I'm not too sure about that. That's in the hands of Colonel Parker, my manager. I'll tell you one thing though, we're landing at Prestwick Airport in Scotland shortly for refuelling, so if you guys could get up there, I'll be glad to meet you and shake you by the hand. Over.'

Eddie shook his head and stared into the heavens.

'It's too late. Prestwick's a long way from here. If we'd known earlier though, we'd have come. Wouldn't we, Jet?'

Jet nodded vigorously.

'Definitely. We'd have got there somehow.'

Then, reverting to Elvis:

'That's a Goddamn shame. Anyhow, if ever you're in Memphis, stop by and see me in Graceland. You'll be mighty welcome. Over.'

'Thanks. That'd be fantastic. Over.'

'OK. I gotta go now. It's been real good talking to you guys. Goodbye now. Over and out.'

'Bye, Elvis! Hope to see you some day. Bye.'

The boys waved up into the darkness, then stood silently, listening to the sound of the engines fade into the distance.

Eddie blinked away his tears and wiped his eyes on the back of his hand. He was travelling along a duel carriageway through a nondescript landscape of farmland and industrial estates.

'It's not far now, kid. We're nearly there.'

When they'd saved up. When they'd won the pools. When they'd robbed a bank. When they'd married an heiress. When they'd held the Queen to ransom, that was when they were going to buy a Cadillac and make the pilgrimage to Prestwick Airport, to commemorate the only occasion that Elvis set foot on British soil.

He passed a road sign – Prestwick Airport 2 mls – then turned off the dual carriageway on to the approach road and saw the airport buildings in the distance. Suddenly, a low-flying aircraft overshadowed him as it came in to land.

'Fucking hell!' Eddie roared, ducking and glancing sky-wards. 'We've made it kid! We're there!'

But when he crossed the flyover and saw the terminal build-ing, imagination wasn't enough any more, he wanted Jet there, beside him, to celebrate their triumphant arrival together.

Eddie parked the car and stared tearfully through the windscreen towards the departure lounge as he relived the series of events which had shattered any hope of fulfilling their dream.

Eddie ran to the bus stop, still shaken after his violent confrontation with Jack. But it was his mother's fault too! If she hadn't insisted on jiving with him, he would have left the house before Jack arrived home. Now he was late. Extremely late. He had arranged to meet Pearl outside the Alhambra at eight o'clock and it was a quarter past already. He stood at the bus stop, staring down the road, willing a bus to appear round the bend. If one arrived immediately he would be in town by half past, and at the cinema by twenty-five to . . . He turned his back on the queue and mouthed a prayer.

Please God, if you send a bus straight away, I'll go to church every Sunday from now on. Honest.

It wasn't much of a request. It wasn't as if he was asking him to part the Red Sea or anything major like that. But five minutes later, God still hadn't obliged and Eddie couldn't stay put any longer. He ran to the next bus stop, glancing back continually in case one approached and he had to make a desperate sprint to catch it. After a short rest, he completed another leg. At least he felt he was getting somewhere, even if it was in vain.

The next stretch was the longest on the route. He pictured it, calculating the distance in his mind. Past the rec. and the clothing factory. Then up the hill past the Cross Keys. It was risky. If he got caught in no-man's-land, he could be in trouble. He kept glancing back, tense and jittery like a relay runner waiting to receive the baton. One minute, two . . . He didn't know what to do. If he set off now and a bus was on its way, he would have wasted two precious minutes, which meant that he might not reach the next stop in time. But if he waited, and one didn't turn up for ages, there would be no point in going into town anyway because Pearl would have gone.

He made a dash for it. He had nothing to lose. It was important to cover the first part of the distance fast, so that if a bus did arrive, he would have a good start. After a two-hundred yard sprint, Eddie was out of breath and exhausted, but thinking about Pearl kept him going. He could see her standing in front of the film poster on the steps of the Alhambra, glancing up and down the road. His vision was interrupted by a dog running out at him. Eddie kicked it in the jaw without breaking stride. He was sweating and gasping for breath and his Brylcreemed pompadour had collapsed and was lashing about his face. An old woman leaving the off-licence, who had read recently of the latest threat to civilization posed by the Teddy-boy craze, suddenly saw one running towards her. The sight of his deranged and desperate appearance confirmed her worst fears and she collapsed on the pavement. Eddie had no idea that he had caused her to faint, but his brothel creepers gave him good lift-off and he hurdled her cleanly without inflicting further harm.

If the pensioner's worst fear was being attacked by a Teddy boy, Eddie's was being caught between bus stops. He glanced round. No! Perhaps it was a lorry. The vehicle was still too far away to identify precisely behind the glare of its headlights. He ran harder, panicking, looked round again. He could make out the lighted upper deck as it approached him. He waved his arms like a drowning man, but the bus sailed past. Eddie slowed down, cursing the driver to hell and back.

Then he noticed that the bus was still standing at the stop. Was the driver waiting for him? Or was it a final, cruel trick to raise his hopes, then drive off as he drew near? Eddie started to run again, but warily, in case he was disappointed. The matter was settled by the conductress appearing on the platform at the back of the bus and beckoning to him.

'Come on, if you're coming! We haven't got all night, you know!'

Eddie sprinted and pulled himself on to the platform with the pole. As he walked down the aisle, panting and dishevelled, a man nudged his mate and pointed to him.

'Hey up! It's Roger Bannister!'

The other passengers laughed, but more galling than their sarcasm was the sight of the people who had been waiting at the first bus stop, smirking at him as he flopped down in his seat.

When Eddie reached the Alhambra, Pearl had gone. He looked up at the town-hall clock. It was ten minutes to nine. Who could blame her? He looked up and down the road, then through the glass doors into the foyer and was immediately transported back to his childhood, when his mother worked here as an usherette. He could see her in her scarlet uniform, tearing tickets by the inner doors with the porthole windows.

Eddie stood on the steps in front of the film poster wondering what to do next. He felt desperate. What if she thought he'd stood her up and wrote him a letter saying that she didn't want to see him again? The prospect turned his stomach and made him feel sick. Thinking about Pearl brightened his days at work, and when he went to bed after a night out together, he hugged his perfumed shirt like a teddy bear.

But where was she now? At home, he hoped, planning to meet him tomorrow. He considered going to her house. He had walked her home a couple of times, then parted after a kiss at the front gate, but they hadn't been seeing each other long enough for him to be introduced to her parents, and he would feel stupid if he knocked on the door and she wasn't in . . . Wasn't in? *Wasn't in*! Where the hell was she then? He felt weak. What if she had stood *him* up and gone out with somebody else? He stared down the road, willing her to appear. She would wave when she saw him, then lean on him out of breath . . . *Sorry I'm late but my mother's broken her leg and I had to take her to hospital* . . . The courting couples walking by with their arms around each other heightened his misery and, when the town-hall clock struck nine, Eddie finally gave up hope and walked away down the High Street, looking into the lighted shop windows and wondering what to do next.

If he went home, he would only mope around sulking and getting on his mother's nerves. He decided to call in at the Cats Eyes to see if Jet, or anybody else he knew, was there.

Jet *was* there. He was down in the basement jiving with Pearl. Eddie had glanced around the coffee bar without recognizing anyone, then passed through the door into the basement and stood at the top of the stairs, scanning the dance floor below. And there they were, rocking together by the juke box to 'All Shook Up'. Eddie certainly was. He felt faint and gripped the banister to steady himself. His girlfriend and best mate betraying him so brazenly.

Pearl saw him first and waved. She pointed him out to Jet, who beckoned to him to come down. They looked pleased to see him but Eddie remained stubbornly on the stairs. Then it happened. Quickly without warning. The record ended. Pearl left Jet and crossed the dance floor but before she reached the stairs, 'Heartbreak Hotel' struck up on the juke box and a boy asked her to dance. She shook her head. He grabbed her arm. She knocked it away. They argued. Jet ran over, pushed the boy away. Threatening each other. The boy's mate joined in. Scuffling. Dark suits merging in the gloom. Tables and chairs crashing over. Dancers scattering. Girls screaming . . . *Oh baby so lonely, baby. Oh baby so lonely, baby* . . . Jet up against the wall. Fists going in. Hit the fucker. That's it. Let him have it, Eddie urged silently from the top of the stairs. Then, as Pearl struggled to drag them off, Jet staggered back on to the juke box and closed down 'Heartbreak Hotel'. His attackers stepped back as Jet dropped to his knees, holding his stomach, and Pearl's scream, when she saw the spreading stain on his white shirt, broke Eddie's trance.

'Jet! Jet!'

He fought his way down the stairs against the tide of the escaping crowd, then dashed across the floor and knelt down beside Pearl, who was sobbing hysterically and holding Jet's hand.

'What's happened? What they done?'

'He stabbed me. The bastard stabbed me.'

'Somebody phone an ambulance!' Eddie shouted.

Jet raised his head and looked down at himself. The blood was spreading over his shirt like spilled ink on a blotter.

'Jesus. I look like a stuck pig.'

Pearl wiped his face with her handkerchief.

'Jet. Jet. Jet.'

He closed his eyes, gasping for breath. Eddie patted his arm.

'Come on kid, wake up. Don't go to sleep.'

Eddie looked round desperately for help, but those who had stayed behind remained at a distance, looking on.

'Do you want some music on? I'll play a record. What do you want?'

Jet opened his eyes and tried to smile.

'Yeah. Great. How about, "Teenage Heaven"?'

Eddie bit his lip to stop himself from laughing. He couldn't see for tears.

'You're going to be all right, kid. It's not as bad as it looks. You know, it's like when you cut yourself shaving and you think you've cut your throat and when it's stopped it's only a nick.' He was babbling, trying to keep Jet awake. 'A few stitches and you'll be as right as rain. Jack said that in Burma some of the men used to get terrible wounds and there were no MOs but they used to get better . . . Jet. Jet.' Eddie patted his hand. 'Open your eyes, Jet. Don't go to sleep.' Jet blinked up at him, trying to focus. 'That's it, kid. Hang on. When you're better, we'll have a piss-up to celebrate. We'll visit every pub in town. We'll get paralytic. It'll be great. Then we'll go to Scotland like we said. We'll buy a Cadi. Go to Prestwick. Remember, Jet? Remember what we said? It'll be fantastic. We'll have a great time.' He shook Jet's sleeve. 'Elvis. Are you reading me?'

Jet opened his eyes and gripped Eddie's hand.

'Yeah . . . Reading you loud and clear, you ole hillbilly cat. This is Elvis, Elvis over England. Over and out.'

Pearl squeezed Jet's hand.

'I'll go and see if the ambulance is coming. Try to hurry it up.'

Eddie watched her run across the room and up the stairs.

'It'll not be long now, kid. It'll soon be here.'

But when he looked down again, Jet was lying still with his head on one side.

'Jet! Jet! Wake up!'

Eddie shook him and slapped his face, but when he raised him up, Jet was limp in his arms.

Eddie sat sobbing with his head resting on the steering-wheel.

'I'm sorry, kid. I know I should have helped. But how did I know that was going to happen? I was jealous. I thought she was two-timing me. How was I to know she'd gone there to wait for me in case I turned up? It was bad luck. Sheer bad luck, that's all.'

People, attracted by the Cadillac as they crossed the car park towards the departure lounge, were embarrassed by the sight of the weeping driver and hurried by. Gradually, Eddie calmed down and raised his head.

'Well, kid, we're here. It's not how we planned it, but we finally made it.'

He wiped his eyes and blew his nose, then got out of the car and locked the door. It was cool and drizzly and mist obscured the runway behind the high wire fence. He crossed the car park, passed the taxi ranks and entered the departure lounge, which was busy with tourists, dressed mainly in leisure outfits more suited to their sunny destinations than the dank, Scottish morning.

As he was studying the departure board, an announcement over the PA informed passengers of the late arrival of the Belfast flight, and would Mr Alan McIntyre please report to gate number 2, where his wife was waiting for him. Poor bastard, Eddie thought, watching a pale man wearing a sombrero and a football shirt sprinting across the concourse, cheered on by a gang of young men in kilts: in trouble already and they haven't even taken off yet.

Then, looking round for a café, he saw it, the sign above the airport bar, GRACELAND, in flowing neon letters. It had crossed his mind that there might be a commemorative plaque somewhere to mark Elvis's landing, but not a gaudy American-style bar. He walked across and looked through the plate glass window, then went in. It was like entering an Elvis museum. The walls were decorated with framed photographs of Elvis in concert and posters of Elvis gigs in Jacksonville, Florida, and the Memorial Auditorium in Buffalo, NY, 21 January 1956: the year of Elvis's first smash hit, 'Heartbreak Hotel'. There was a street sign — MEMPHIS ELVIS PRESLEY BLVD; an Elvis numberplate — TENNESSEE 1-ELVIS MEMPHIS; and a wall-hanging like the one in Sue's cottage, of Elvis wearing a white jump suit with a garland of red flowers around his neck.

Eddie read an old cutting from a local newspaper about

Elvis landing at Prestwick, then studied the grainy photo-graph of Elvis in uniform, flanked by two grinning youths with sideburns and greased-back hair. Eddie shook his head, ruefully.

'That could have been us, kid, if only we'd known.'

He bought a bottle of Bud, then selected a record on the juke box in the corner of the bar. As Elvis sang 'Crying In The Chapel', Eddie stood up straight with his Bud by his side and his head bowed, pretending that he was looking at the framed ticket to Graceland, hanging low down on the wall.

'It's taken us a long time, kid,' he whispered. 'But we finally made it.'

But now that it was all over, he felt lonely and sad. When the record ended, he sat down at a table overlooking the lounge and considered his next move. The thought of going home and confronting Pearl filled him with dread. He couldn't imagine her welcoming him back with open arms. Firearms perhaps, but not the loving kind. He stared morosely through the window at the departure board. The light beside the Chicago flight was flashing red and indicating BOARDING . . . Chicago. State capital of Illinois. His father came from Illinois, a town called Springfield, two hundred miles from Chicago. Eddie closed his eyes and saw the red road on the map, running south. He wondered what had become of him. Had he been killed during the war, as his mother always maintained? Or did he survive and return home? Perhaps he was still alive. Tears filled Eddie's eyes, as he saw himself hugging a leathery old critter in bib and braces on the porch of a wooden house. Perhaps he had half brothers and sisters over there?

Then he thought of something which took his breath away. Why didn't he go and find out? He was so overwhelmed by the notion that he needed another beer to settle himself down and think it through.

He had already decided that there wasn't much to go home for, and the break would give them a chance to decide on their future plans. How much would the flight cost? How long could he afford to stay? He might have to sell the car, but now the pilgrimage was over, it didn't seem as important any more. He was almost packed and ready to go, when he thought of something else. A passport! He didn't have a passport! But he came up with a solution which made him even more determined to go ahead with his plan. He would go back and stay at the pub opposite Sue's cottage until he had made the arrangements.

He watched the changing destinations on the departure board, then, tossing his mother's silver dollar, he left the Graceland Bar and crossed the concourse to the flight information desk.